soft landing

a novel

LAUREL HERMANSON

CAPER PRESS

Copyright © 2009 by Laurel Hermanson

All rights reserved. No part of this book may be reproduced in any form or by any electronic or mechanical means, including information storage and retrieval systems, without permission in writing from the publisher, except by a reviewer who may quote brief passages in a review.

 CAPER PRESS

Visit our websites at www.caperpress.com
or www.laurelhermanson.com

The characters and events in this book are fictitious. Any similarity to real persons, living or dead, is coincidental and not intended by the author.

ISBN 978-0-557-04574-7

Printed in the United States of America

Cover design by Jay Mauricio
Cover photo © JupiterImages

For Mom & Dad

soft landing

PROLOGUE

In a city of more than eight million people, no one sees the old man jump. He plods along the south walkway of the Brooklyn Bridge, puffing and wheezing until he reaches its midpoint. He grips the railing and leans to catch his breath. Straightening, he wipes his brow with a crisp, white handkerchief, which he folds neatly and returns to his pocket.

He smoothes his hair, straightens his suit coat and faces west to contemplate the Statue of Liberty. He saw it for the first time seventy years ago, when he was five. He is somewhat surprised to find it still inspires awe, and now, something more — gratitude, tempered by nostalgia. His gaze drifts, settling on the giants of the financial district, before he turns north toward Midtown South and studies the Empire State Building. After the proliferation of skyscrapers in the late twenties and early thirties, these behemoths were still new upon his arrival. The country was in a depression, however, and like countless jobless workers, many buildings stood empty and unused, hence nicknames such as the Empty State Building.

Later came the Twin Towers. He always felt fortunate to have witnessed their ascent, but he sometimes wishes he hadn't lived to see their destruction. There are no ruins, as there are in Italy. Rather, the Americans made quick work of clearing away all evidence that the buildings existed at all. He hears talk of a memorial, but he can't imagine one that will do justice to all that was lost. He sighs, not wanting his last thoughts to be of death and tragedy. He doesn't want to feel sadness or anger. There is too much good to remember.

He stands now where he proposed to his wife forty-five years ago. This is where she told him they were expecting their first child a year later, and their second two years after that. This is where he scattered her ashes three years ago to the day. He has lived a good life, a life of which he is proud. Until very recently he never felt old, but now he is sick. He is dying, in fact. Now he is ready to join the woman he has loved for so long and whom he misses so desperately. His affairs are in order. He is done.

It is very early morning. The few passersby pay little attention to an old man sightseeing. Climbing over the railing is much easier than he expected, considering the weights in his pockets. Without hesitation, he spreads his arms and takes his final step.

CHAPTER ONE

Maxine Reise is not especially comfortable around children, yet here she is. The neighborhood around Marina Bay is a sea of kids, as if an extension of the bay itself. Children are everywhere: scampering in the streets, pushing their way through the crowded sidewalks, towering overhead on their fathers' shoulders, even tiny reflections of kids in the hopeful, eager eyes of Maxine's fiancé, Michael Silver. The annual children's parade is about to start, so this is to be expected, but Maxine is rattled nonetheless.

Michael dragged Maxine to the parade, ostensibly to help her feel more a part of their new community. Six months after arriving here, however, Kirkland feels about as much like home as, say, Reykjavik. She suspects this child immersion exercise is also the most recent tactic in another ongoing campaign. She watches Michael as he takes in the chaotic scene, clearly enjoying himself. He squeezes her hand now and then, laughing every time another youngster slams into them. Not wanting to disappoint, Maxine grins and nods.

Slowly the street clears and the crowd quiets. Heads turn in anticipation as a cacophony of drums and horns precedes the first group of kids, a middle school marching band. As the band rounds a corner several blocks away and makes its way toward them, Maxine studies the spectators. With a few variations, the moms wear khakis, loafers, expensive-looking sweaters and bright windbreakers.

This explains why Michael, as they were leaving the house, asked if she needed a minute to change. Believing he was worried she would be cold, Maxine added a bright chartreuse scarf. Now, in her black jeans, scuffed boots and suede jacket, she is a bit self-conscious and wishes he'd been more specific.

The fathers are fewer in number and many are wearing suits, presumably taking a break from work, even though it's a holiday. Maxine wonders what it is she finds so appealing about a good looking man in a business suit holding a child. She supposes it provides a nurturing, selfless quality that might otherwise be lacking. She glances at Michael and tries to shoehorn him into this scenario. She shivers and stuffs her hands in her pockets. Despite the fact that it is the Fourth of July, the temperature hovers somewhere in the sixties, and the stubborn wind makes Maxine's eyes water. A layer of bruised clouds blankets the bay, spewing occasional angry warnings, yet nobody else appears to be thinking this is a perfectly shitty day for a parade.

The band marches noisily by. Maxine thinks they look less like small soldiers than big toy soldiers come to life, serious and intent, with overly simple uniforms and shoes. At the very least, they must be happy to be warm.

The drill team isn't so lucky. Eggplant-colored unitards with swirling bell-bottoms are all that stand between these poor girls and the hostile weather. The thin, shiny material can't offer much warmth, the dark color and clingy texture serving instead to exaggerate the girls' pale skin and pudgy midsections as they dip and twirl their huge flags.

Maxine nudges Michael and says, "Drill team's never the best looking bunch, is it?"

Michael looks at her oddly and turns away. Maxine glances around. Did she speak too loudly? She would expect at least a conspiratorial shush if he were simply afraid someone might overhear. More likely, her editing mechanism has again failed to adequately screen her thoughts on their way from her brain to her mouth. Not a complete failure to engage, however; her brain proffered the words: *ugly kids*. The thought crept in uninvited and will not go away just because she doesn't like it. Like an annoying relative in one's living room, smoking cigars during an unannounced visit, "ugly kids" will stink up the place long after it has been shown the door.

Maxine's mental sieve becomes finer with each blunder, but she occasionally worries about its endurance. She has a fleeting vision of a dryer going up in flames, a faulty lint trap the presumable culprit, but the lazy owner the real transgressor. Sloth is her favorite of the deadly sins, but not the real problem here. How does one clean out one's brain?

A dozen preschool kids march past. The common element in their outfits seems to be alien antennae with bouncing, sparkly balls. Organized in messy rows of three, this ragtag bunch draws enthusiastic whistles and applause from the crowd. Maxine sees several moms waving, calling out names and laughing gaily. Maternal pride, perhaps combined with sleep deprivation, could explain this behavior among the mothers. Michael, however, also laughs and claps as if this is the cleverest display he's ever seen. He is more delighted, in fact, than most of the fathers in the crowd, who appear dazed and preoccupied.

Am I missing something? Maxine rubs her eyes and forehead absently.

Michael glances at her. "Headache?"

"Little one," Maxine replies.

Michael reaches into the inside breast pocket of his coat and hands Maxine a small foil packet. She takes it from him with some surprise, liberating a pill and placing it under her tongue. Gratitude and a hint of irritation join the dull ache behind her eyes.

His office is closed for the holiday, but Michael wants to stop by to catch up on paperwork. Not wanting to hang around, Maxine declines his offer of a ride home in favor of getting some exercise. As she hurries toward home, dodging groups of unruly kids and frazzled parents, her mind is already in work mode, mulling over the particulars of a calculation that has been giving her problems all morning. She is eager to be done with her current project, a relatively simple invoicing program, but last minute details threaten to delay its completion. She has bid on a more ambitious database project and wants to be free to give it her full attention if her proposal is accepted.

Soft Landing

Maxine turns onto a street off the parade route, mercifully free of crowds. She relaxes a little and begins to notice the houses lining the block. The impression is one of affluence and excruciating tidiness. Hard to tell where the Joneses live on this street. Their own street is much the same, and since they moved into their house, Maxine and Michael have debated the scope of work that will need to be done before their front yard measures up to its neighbors. Maxine always dreamed of having green space of her own to beautify, but it turns out gardening is far more appealing in theory than in reality. Michael is convinced Maxine could be a brilliant gardener if she just gave it some time, but she finds it intimidating and has concluded landscaping is best left to professionals. She would prefer to focus her efforts on a vegetable garden in the back yard, but this has been put off until the front is deemed presentable.

Job one was decorating the interior of the house. Maxine was happy once they had furniture and her books were unpacked, but Michael had a vision and pursued it diligently until it was realized. He chose what he called an eclectic blend of contemporary upholstered furniture and antique wooden pieces, along with a sophisticated but spare collection of art and accessories. There is no question it is lovely, and Michael keeps it spotless and tidy. Actually, he pays a woman to clean once a week, which makes Maxine uncomfortable, since she works from home. Should she stay home and move to a different room when Blanca, who speaks very little English, is ready to clean her office? Should she vacate the house altogether? Mostly, Maxine tries to stay out of the way, and she and Blanca nod and smile at one another when their paths cross. Cleaning lady or no cleaning lady, Maxine wishes it felt less like a page from a shelter magazine and more like a home, the kind of place that made you want to kick back with a good book and a cup of coffee and wile away an afternoon. Maxine suspects the house would prefer to host hip friends for cocktails and canapés, except they have no hip friends, or unhip friends, for that matter.

    Maxine spots a "For Sale" sign across the street in front of a striking, contemporary house. She slows to envy the lush garden. Cheery black-eyed Susans and soothing lavender contrast with the blood red of prickly barberry; lilac trees heavy with fragrant purple blossoms arch over showy white lilies and spidery ornamental grasses. *That doesn't look so hard.* Maxine is startled out of her reverie by a man leading a dark-haired little girl around the side of the house and into the back yard. The man's back is to her, but the little girl catches her eye for a moment before she disappears from view.

    Maxine continues walking, but something in the girl's eyes causes her to slow, and then stop. She turns back toward the house and stares at the spot where they just were. She takes a few tentative steps toward the house and stops again, looking up and down the empty street. After a few seconds of indecision, she strolls over to the realtor's sign and pulls a listing sheet from the plastic box attached to the post, noting the steep asking price and generous square footage. She steps to the side of the house and makes her way along a stone path toward the back yard.

    Rounding the corner of the house, Maxine holds the flyer conspicuously in front of her and affects what she hopes is a friendly, curious expression. No one is in sight. The back yard is empty, save for a few squirrels chasing each other in the branches of a huge old cherry tree. One of them chatters loudly, and Maxine jumps.

This is beautiful. Maxine admires the porch that stretches the length of the house, complete with three sets of French doors. The doors closest to her offer a view into a corner room, illuminated by windows on the side of the house and, as far as Maxine can tell, empty. Glancing toward the center doors, she notices a lockbox hanging open from the door handle. *Huh.* Most likely, this man is the girl's father, or a relative, or a family friend and this is their house for sale. Maybe they were at the parade and the girl needed to pee, and she just couldn't wait until they got to their new home. Maybe he's a realtor and he wanted to check it out while they were in the neighborhood. There are countless reasonable explanations.

Maxine tries to get a look inside the middle set of doors, but the interior is dim and all she sees is the top half of herself, furtive and unsure, reflected in the glass. Irritated by this specter, she climbs the porch steps and presses her face to the glass. Seeing nothing but an empty dining room with several lovely built-ins and another empty room beyond, she steps back and turns to her right.

A stunning rose-covered arbor extends from above the third set of doors. Maxine ponders what a moody bitch the rose is. Michael swears that the Pacific Northwest is the ideal climate in which to grow roses, but Maxine's attempts have yielded little but disappointment and the dreaded black spot. She pauses and buries her nose in a bloom as she passes by.

The last set of doors leads into a bright, country-style kitchen. Cupping her hands around her face for a better look, Maxine thinks this room could use some updating, given the price tag. Across the kitchen is a long breakfast bar, and beyond that, a family room. As her eyes adjust to the light, Maxine sees the back of what appears to be the single remaining piece of furniture, a slip-covered sofa, upon which are seated two figures. The man's back is to Maxine, but the little girl sits sideways, her expression blank, her dark eyes fixed on a point in the distance, a million miles from what's happening here. Maxine takes in the way the man leans back into the cushions, how one shoulder moves slightly, rhythmically.

Maxine springs back as if the door suddenly delivered an electric shock, and for a moment remains motionless. Slowly she approaches the door again, certain that she was mistaken, that the funky lighting and migraine medication are playing tricks with her vision and her suspicious nature. She cups her hands around her eyes again and squints hard, willing herself to see something more acceptable, but the scene is unchanged.

Maxine backs slowly away from the door, a familiar shroud of denial encircling her brain, slithering down her spine and leaving her body feeling dull and paralyzed. She stares at her reflection accusingly. *Do something.*

She backs down the porch steps, slowly and clumsily. She pats her pockets but can visualize her cell phone on the kitchen counter, attached to its charger. She lumbers around the side of the house and glances at the sprawling ranch next door, then crosses the neighboring yard and climbs the steps to the front porch. She rings the doorbell, but she can tell by the complete stillness that nobody will answer. She waits for what seems an eternity before giving up.

Back at the mostly empty house, Maxine trudges up the steps and stops before the front door, still under the spell of fear and uncertainty. She watches her hand reach out and press the doorbell politely. Having crossed this line, something inside Maxine snaps. She rings again, this time punching the button repeatedly. When nothing happens after a full minute, she bangs the door with her fist.

"Hello!" Her shout sounds weak and hollow to her own ears. She reaches for the bell again, gives it a jab, balls up her fist and raises her arm to knock again. The door swings suddenly and violently open, and she snatches back her hand.

The man in front of her does not look like a pedophile. He appears quite distinguished, pushing forty with graying hair and an expensive suit. Not really her style, but tall and fit and well put-together. He's also quite cheerful.

"Hey!" he exclaims with a big smile and wide eyes, as if Maxine is an old friend he couldn't be happier to see. His eyes dart to the flyer in Maxine's hand. "Sorry, but if you want to see the house, you'll have to make an appointment."

Maxine stares at him, the reality of this large man and her utter lack of a plan almost extinguishing her adrenaline high. Maxine's eyes widen as she looks behind him. "Oh, but this is fantastic!" The man turns and looks in the direction of her gaze, giving Maxine enough room to squeeze past. Maxine barges into the foyer, gawking like a country girl in a big city for the first time.

"Hey!" he cries again, still upbeat, but when Maxine glances at him, she sees his smile is strained. She grins back nervously and continues looking around. The family room is off to Maxine's left, and she sees the little girl standing in front of the couch staring at her. Maxine stops in her tracks and stares back. The girl is significantly taller than the kids in the kindergarten class at the parade, so Maxine figures she's six or seven, maybe eight.

"Hi there. What's your name?" Maxine thinks her voice sounds a bit hysterical and doesn't blame the girl for not answering. She turns back to the man, who takes several steps in her direction.

"Like I said, this isn't a good time. I'm expecting a client any minute." His voice is chillier, but the smile is still stretched tight across his face.

Maxine turns and takes a few steps toward the girl. "I'm Maxine. What's your name?" When the girl still doesn't reply, Maxine asks, "Everything okay here?"

"What do you think you're doing?" Surprised by the sudden hostility in the man's voice, Maxine spins around, and when she sees the look in his eyes, she reflexively steps back. A surge of anger almost immediately replaces her uncertainty.

"What are *you* doing?" Maxine's voice shakes. He mistakes her rage for fear and tries to intimidate her, puffing up like a blowfish and moving a few steps closer to her. Maxine giggles involuntarily, and sees a hint of alarm creep into his eyes.

"Are you crazy? Get out of here or I'll call the

police." He grabs Maxine's arm. She's not sure whether he intends to hurt her or simply to usher her out. Either way, it's a mistake on his part. Without hesitation, Maxine knees him in the groin, freeing herself from his grip. As he doubles over in pain, Maxine recognizes this as her last chance to run away. For a moment, she lets the idea bounce deliciously around the inside of her head, hating herself. Briefly, she binges on cowardice, all the while knowing she won't stomach it, not this time.

Maxine hurries into the family room and reaches for the little girl's arm. The child, terrified, pulls away. Maxine cocks her head and peers at her, perplexed.

Maxine pleads under her breath, "It's okay — "

"Get away from her!" Maxine turns. The man still isn't standing up straight, but he stumbles into the room holding his groin, his face purple.

Maxine has wanted to kick someone like him for as long as she can remember. Not just a knee to the balls, but a real power kick to the chin. As he moves toward her, she backs up, thinking his head is at the perfect height. She takes a few tentative hops up and down and delivers a kick intended for his lower left jaw. She's slow and off balance, though, and he sees it coming. He feints to the right, and her foot barely connects with his left shoulder, causing him more confusion than pain.

He stares at her, his eyes wide. "You're a goddamn lunatic." He straightens up a little more, wincing, and turns his attention to the girl. The corners of his mouth twitch into a smile. He reaches out a hand and murmurs, "It's okay, honey, I won't let her hurt you." The little girl might as well be made of stone. Maxine thinks she sees his eyes darken as he says, "Oh for God's sake — "

Maxine takes advantage of his focus on the girl and tries again. This time she's dead on. His head snaps to the side and his knees buckle. He crumples to the floor slowly, his fall ending with the thud of his head against the nicely refinished hardwood floor.

Her adrenaline spiking wildly, Maxine takes a few deep breaths to regain control. She looks up and sees the little girl rooted to the same spot, looking back and forth from Maxine to the man on the floor, her mouth hanging open and her dark eyes huge. Maxine's victorious smile vanishes. She unclenches her fists and tries to shed her fighting posture, shaking her head and arms to loosen up.

"Are you okay?" This seems like an idiotic question. "What's your name?" Still no reply. They stare at each other while Maxine considers her next move. "I swear I'm not going to hurt you — "

The man groans, and Maxine and the little girl both jump. Maxine decides she can't wait any longer and grabs the girl's arm, pulling her out the front door and down the steps. The child offers no resistance as they hurry down the street.

They reach the end of the block and Maxine looks back, half expecting to see the man running after them. The street is as deserted as it was before. She leads the girl around the corner onto a side street so they won't be in plain sight if he does come looking for them. Maxine now realizes that, while she may have overcome the immediate threat, getting the girl out of the house is just the beginning.

"What's your name?" The girl stares at her. "You

know I'm not going to hurt you, right?" A long pause, then a barely perceptible nod. Maxine sighs, relieved to no longer feel like part of the problem. "Do you live close to here?" Another nod. "Okay. Can you find your house from here?" The girl looks around helplessly, turning back to Maxine with tears in her eyes. Maxine feels a little like crying herself. "It's okay, we'll get you home." It occurs to her that this might not be the most comforting thought. "That man — he's not your father, is he?" The girl shakes her head. "And you don't live with him, do you?" Shake.

Maxine takes her hand and leads her in the direction of her own home, not having any idea where to take a stray, molested, mute child. As she wonders where the local police station might be, Maxine feels the child tug her hand. Maxine turns, and the little girl whispers, "Chloe."

Maxine stops and stares down, her heart breaking. "Okay, Chloe. I'm Maxine." Chloe nods gravely, and they continue walking. *Okay, not mute, just stray and molested.*

Michael has been irritable all afternoon, and he's afraid his performance with his patients has suffered as a result. Between sessions, he's tried unsuccessfully to put his finger on what is bothering him. While he's quite adept at getting even the most reluctant child to define and confront their emotional struggles, it's a skill he himself, at the age of thirty-four, hasn't quite mastered, and this knowledge aggravates his mood.

Michael's spirits lift as he sinks into the plush leather interior of his BMW. He can feel his body and brain relax as he begins the short trip home. A good jazz CD and the incredibly responsive handling of this superb car are all it takes to help him transition from work, where he must be ever vigilant, to a comfortable evening at home with Maxine, his beautiful fiancée, whom he believes benefits from his calm, stable presence.

Michael is thinking about Maxine as he pulls onto the highway, navigating the sharply curved entrance ramp expertly with a series of downshifts but no braking, then accelerating out of the turn with a mental nod to German engineering. He wonders if she enjoyed the parade as much as he did, although he suspects she resented being dragged away from work and therefore didn't give it a chance. He wishes she were more open with him, rather than succumbing to such passive-aggressive tendencies.

Also worrisome are Maxine's migraines, their frequency and intensity having become increasingly disruptive to their daily lives. Michael hasn't mentioned this to Maxine, but he's beginning to discern a pattern in the timing of her headaches. He doesn't believe she's faking it, of course, but it seems as though activities Maxine finds stressful or distasteful — social gatherings, functions related to his job, yard work — usually precipitate a headache. Of course, there are exceptions, but Michael feels obligated to explore this possible connection.

Michael makes a final turn onto his block. As he draws near his house, he sees a police cruiser pulling away from the curb in front. An unmarked sedan is parked in his driveway, blocking access to the garage. He parks on the street, hops out and hurries up the front walk, his drive-time calm long gone.

Opening the front door, Michael sees nothing but an empty living room. "Maxine?" No response, but he hears voices. He drops his coat onto a chair and strides through the dining room.

He finds them in the kitchen. Maxine and a strange man sit at the kitchen table, while a woman leans on the counter jotting notes on a pad. Both are dressed in plain clothes. All three look up at him as though they haven't heard him hollering all over the house.

"Michael." Maxine seems particularly surprised to see him, and oblivious to the fact that the presence of police cars outside his home might cause him to fear something had happened to her, or to the house. The man stands as if waiting to be introduced. He's tall, well over six feet, and absurdly fit. Michael feels like a junior high school kid standing next to him.

"What the hell is going on?" Michael hears the irritation in his voice and tries to soften it. "Are you alright?"

"I'm fine." Maxine stands. "These are detectives Hancock and — ?" She turns to the woman, who pockets her pad and pen and smiles.

"Laird." She's petite, a foot and a half shorter than her partner, who seems like a giant standing between her and Maxine.

"We'll be in touch," the giant says in a deep bass. "Like I said, it'll be up to the DA whether or not to press charges. Call me if you think of anything else." He smiles and hands a card to Maxine, who nods somberly.

"Yes sir." Michael is certain he has never heard Maxine call anyone "sir" before. On her best behavior, she exhibits an unmistakable disdain for authority figures. He wonders what this one has done to earn her esteem.

"You kicked him again?" Michael stares at Maxine in disbelief. He's trying to let her finish, as she has requested numerous times, but this is too much to process all at once.

"What was I supposed to do? God knows what he would have done next." After a pause, Michael nods as if he understands, although clearly he does not.

Maxine sighs, deflated. "Anyway, he dropped like a stone and then Chloe and I came here and I called the cops." Maxine turns away and there is a long silence. "God, Michael, you should have seen her face when I walked in. She just looked so... guilty."

If he didn't know her better, Michael might think she was about to cry. "What did the cop mean about pressing charges?"

"Well, apparently the man is her uncle or something and he's claiming I just barged in and assaulted him for no reason."

Michael cocks his head and frowns. "For no reason? Is he kidding? What about what he was... doing to her?"

Maxine shrugs. "She wouldn't tell the police anything other than her name, so for now it's my word against his."

Michael nods, pleased to be discussing a topic with which he is professionally acquainted. "She'll open up eventually, with the right guidance. They almost always do." He pauses as a thought occurs to him, weighing whether or not to mention it at this time. He decides it's best to pursue it while the incident is still fresh in Maxine's mind. "You're sure about what you saw, aren't you?"

Maxine turns and stares at him. "Jesus Christ, Michael, of course I'm sure. What the hell kind of question is that?" He watches as she pulls herself up from the sofa and disappears upstairs. He can't help but find her defensiveness troublesome. His shoulders feel heavy, a blanket of foreboding settling in and weighing him down.

It all started with a *thunk*. More of a *bonk*, really, but the day the robin started hurling his body against Chloe's bedroom window was the last time things were normal. When Chloe screamed, her mom came running into her room to see what all the fuss was about, and then she laughed and climbed into the twin bed and snuggled with Chloe under the flowery comforter. She told her that in the spring boy robins are so crazy to find a mate that they see their own reflection in a window and think it's another boy robin. So they attack it to keep it from stealing their mate.

That afternoon Chloe and her mom found the nest. They were sitting on the back steps deciding where to plant pansies when a flutter of wings disappeared into a corner of the wisteria arbor. Her dad had built the arbor over one end of the concrete patio. Chloe's mom sighed and said, "Silly mama bird, you can't build your nest over concrete!" Then they cut some branches from the laurel bushes by the fence and piled them under the nest so that if an egg or a baby bird fell out it wouldn't go *splat* on the concrete.

Later Chloe's mom got a phone call from her doctor, which was weird since it was a Saturday. Chloe was sent to her room while her parents talked, and all she heard were words like biopsy results and lumpectomy and radiation. At dinner, her parents explained that one of her mom's breasts was sick and they had to remove the sick part so that it didn't spread. That sounded easy enough to Chloe, but it didn't turn out that way. Chloe pictures their old lives as a pretty drawing on an Etch-A-Sketch, before someone came along and kicked it so that the picture was all wobbly and distorted, like your reflection in a fun house mirror.

That was three months ago. Now Chloe is sitting alone in her bedroom while a bunch of grownups talk quietly downstairs. Well, most of them are quiet. Her mom is really upset, and Chloe can hear her crying, but she can't make out all the words. Just little bits like, "Oh no, no..." and "He couldn't..." but nothing to let her know for sure how bad it is.

She's supposed to be lying down, but Chloe is too wound up, and she has a stomachache. Her mom and dad don't usually let her drink pop, but she had two in a row when she was at Maxine's house, and a bunch of cookies. Maxine is different than any grownup Chloe has met, with her long blond hair and grey suede jacket, and those old black boots.

Chloe hears footsteps on the stairs, and quickly lies down, closing her eyes. Her bedroom door opens, and whoever it is stands in the doorway, sniffling quietly. Footsteps cross to the bed and her mom climbs in behind her, spooning her and wrapping her arms around her and burying her face in Chloe's hair the way she used to. Chloe stirs and breathes deeply as if she's asleep, then lies perfectly still. This is the happiest she has been in three months.

Chloe wakes up in her bedroom and looks around, alone and confused in the fading light. She wants to lie here and pretend that she's still seven and that the last three months never happened, a game she plays a lot since her mom got sick and school let out and Uncle Deon started babysitting. Sometimes she is able to remember whole days spent in the second grade, and review them as if they happened yesterday, but this takes an awful lot of concentration and right now she's really hungry and she needs to pee.

On her way to the bathroom, Chloe sees her parents' closed bedroom door and wonders if her mom has gone back to bed. She hears nothing from downstairs, and as she sits on the toilet, she decides to sneak down to the kitchen and make herself a sandwich. She's been in trouble before, like the time she rode her bike to Haley's house and her mom didn't know where she was, but they've never eaten dinner without her. She feels a tightening at the back of her throat and her eyes sting, but she takes deep breaths until it passes, another trick she's learned this summer.

In the kitchen, Chloe has just gotten together all of the items she needs for a peanut butter and jelly sandwich when her dad flips on the light. She freezes, knife aloft, and stares at him like a dog caught drinking from the toilet.

"Hungry?" He sits with her at the island. He doesn't look mad, just tired, and sad. She nods.

"Me too. How about we go get some pizza?" Chloe's eyes light up. This is not at all what she expected, and she's afraid to trust this sudden hopeful feeling. But pizza's pizza, so she nods enthusiastically.

"Should I go get Mommy?"

"Uh, Mom's napping for a while. Just you and me, okay?"

"Okay." Chloe tries to hide her disappointment from her dad as she carefully screws the cap back on the peanut butter and returns the sandwich fixings to the refrigerator.

Chloe's father is so out of it at the restaurant that he lets her order a hot fudge sundae after eating only one slice of pizza. Between the ordering of the sundae and its arrival, Chloe starts to worry that he might realize what she's done and make her eat another slice while the ice cream melts. Even worse, he could send the sundae back. She starts wolfing down a second slice, hoping she won't be too full to enjoy dessert.

"Chloe, I want to talk to you about the next few days, okay?" Chloe's mouth is full of pizza, so she nods. "Your mom and I want you to talk to someone about... what happened today." He pauses and rubs his eyes, and Chloe realizes she was right, that it isn't over just yet. When her dad looks back at her, her mouth is still full but she's stopped chewing. She looks down at the half-slice in her hand and starts tearing it into little pieces. She wants to spit out what's in her mouth, but makes herself finish chewing it and swallow.

"Hey," her dad says gently. When Chloe looks up, he puts a hand on her arm. "Your mom and I love you like crazy, and we always will, no matter what. You know that, right?"

Chloe nods. He's obviously trying to prepare her for something awful, but just then the waitress appears at the table with her sundae and a box for their leftover pizza. While her dad slides the pizza into the box, Chloe tucks into her ice cream as if it's the last sundae she'll ever eat.

"Chloe." She looks at her dad but doesn't stop shoveling ice cream into her mouth. She's eating it so fast her forehead starts to hurt, but she wants to get through at least the part with hot fudge on it. Her dad smiles a little. "C'est bon?"

"Oui." Chloe smiles back tentatively. Usually, only her mom speaks to her in French, and that's just when she's upset or excited, or if she's had two glasses of wine with dinner. Her dad speaks Italian, but only to his own father, who came to America when he was a little boy.

Her dad watches her for a second. "Chloe, slow down. We're not really in any big hurry." He sounds amused, not at all like he's getting ready to deliver bad news. Chloe slows down, trying to savor every last drop of melting ice cream. Her dad pulls out his wallet and studies the bill, scratching his chin as he figures out the tip. He leaves cash on the little plastic tray and takes the red and white mints, unwrapping one and popping it in his mouth. He drops the other in his shirt pocket. Chloe knows he'll surprise her with it later when she's forgotten all about it.

"So, we want you to talk to someone about what happened, and it's important that you tell her the truth. No matter what anyone else might have said, it's really okay for you to tell this lady everything."

Chloe looks down at her empty bowl and scrapes at it with her spoon.

Her dad pushes the little plastic tray to the edge of the table and folds his hands in front of him. "I also want you to understand that you didn't do anything wrong. You're not in any trouble, okay?"

Chloe continues scraping her bowl, not sure what to say or do. Her father puts a hand under her chin and turns her face until she looks at him.

"You didn't do anything wrong, noodle. You understand that, don't you?"

Chloe nods her head, but her eyes fill with tears and she turns away. She hears her dad sigh, and then he slaps his hands on his thighs.

"Okay. Let's go home."

Maxine lies still, listening peevishly to Michael's gentle snoring. Despite having consumed the better part of a bottle of cabernet and taken an antihistamine, she knows sleep won't come easily tonight. With a resigned sigh, she rolls gently out of bed and pads to the living room. She picks up the novel she's been reading and curls up on the couch, flipping on a lamp. She reads the same sentence half a dozen times, and after a few minutes, the book lies forgotten in her lap. She stares at the blank television screen, her head full of unwanted thoughts.

The year after graduating from college, Maxine lived in a cheap apartment in a rapidly gentrifying neighborhood on the north side of Chicago. Her thirty-something condo-dwelling neighbors insisted they found the area's diversity refreshing as they stepped over used condoms and hypodermic needles on the way to their SUVs. Maxine lived alone in an apartment building that had yet to evict the riffraff and go condo. While she had nothing against diversity, the arrival of affluent young couples had created an uncomfortable tension in the neighborhood. Without an alarm system or even a secure building entrance, safety was an issue, so she took a class in self-defense. With her strong, limber build and relatively low threshold for anger, Maxine was an excellent student. Many times, she found herself hoping for an opportunity to test her skills.

A mugger would have been sufficient. She slides down into the couch cushions, making herself as small as possible. She buries her face in a pillow, trying to squeeze out the image of little girls with scared, pleading eyes.

CHAPTER TWO

Michael awakens to find Maxine's side of the bed empty, which is odd because she's always sound asleep when he gets up. He heads to the bathroom and performs his morning routine without the slightest variation: he pees, brushes his teeth, showers, shaves, puts a little product in his short hair, then grins at the mirror, one eyebrow raised. He walks through the bedroom and into the tidy walk-in closet. Well, his side is tidy. Maxine's space could use a little organizing, particularly her folded clothes. He mentally runs through today's client schedule before choosing olive chinos, a white dress shirt and a beige cotton sweater, all Ralph Lauren. After some deliberation, he selects a black belt and shoes. He picks out a conservative tie but won't put it on until later in the day. He calculates that most of today's clients are fragile and will be more comfortable if he appears casual in a sweater with the top button of his shirt undone. He will remove his sweater, button his shirt and add the tie for one rebellious teenager who he believes will respond better to a more authoritative presence.

Michael glances at Maxine's clothes and makes a mental note to pick up her birthday present today. He was considering a pair of leather driving moccasins, but decided instead on an ivory cashmere tank. He figured shoes were risky to buy without her trying them on, but he couldn't go wrong with cashmere. He can't wait to see it against her tanned shoulders and long, golden hair.

He strides into the living room and finds Maxine sound asleep on the couch, a book clutched to her chest. Maxine has a voracious appetite for literature, which Michael admires. He wishes he had time to read fiction.

"Maxine? Baby?" No response. He feels a small stab of betrayal, as if her leaving their bed implies that sleeping with him, lying next to him at night after a difficult day, isn't enough for her. He wonders if she waited for him to fall asleep so that she could have another drink, but he doesn't see a wine glass anywhere.

Michael hates to wake Maxine, because he always feels that he's done something wrong. No matter how gentle and cheerful his technique, she always behaves like a dog that's been rousted from a sound sleep by having its tail yanked. He worries that someday she'll actually go for his throat. Since he's in a bit of a hurry he decides to let this sleeping beauty lie, and heads into the kitchen.

A fresh pot of coffee awaits him, programmed to finish brewing by seven o'clock every morning. He pours half the carafe into a travel mug, grabs an energy bar from the pantry and retrieves his briefcase and car keys from the foyer. With a final glance at Maxine, he slips out the door.

"Forgive me Father for I have sinned," Maxine intones.

"Uh huh. This had better be good. I'm missing a faculty luncheon as we speak." The boyishly handsome priest sips coffee across the table from Maxine and scans a menu.

"You hate faculty luncheons." Maxine tries to catch the waiter's eye. The diner is close to campus, and even though it's summer session, she wants to order before the lunch rush.

"Hate is such an ugly word. And I certainly have nothing against the lasagna that was to accompany today's meeting." He sets his menu on the edge of the table.

Maxine rolls her eyes. "The free lasagna, you mean. Don't worry, Brian, lunch is on me."

Father Brian is a Catholic priest with whom Maxine grew up in Bozeman. In fact, Maxine is pretty sure they went steady in the fifth grade. They lost touch after high school, but shortly after Maxine and Michael moved to Kirkland she heard from a friend that Brian had accepted a position as assistant to the vice president at Seattle University, a Jesuit Catholic school across Lake Washington on Capitol Hill. Not knowing another soul in town, Maxine had emailed him on a whim. Renewing their friendship was surprisingly easy, particularly since they no longer had anything in common other than their shared childhood and a caustic wit. Of course, she feels that singular comfort and familiarity she could feel only around someone who saw her throw up on her desk in the third grade. Now she finds his company oddly calming and credits him with keeping her sane these last few months.

Their waiter approaches and takes their order

without once actually looking at them. This suits Maxine just fine. Being seen in public with a priest still makes her feel a little self conscious, even though he wears just the collar and a black shirt and trousers. She orders a Cobb salad, then stares in awe as he orders a Reuben, a cup of chicken soup and a slice of pie. Their waiter shuffles away, head down.

"Holy crap, I don't know how you can eat so much. I guess you don't have to worry about letting yourself go when you're not trying to impress the ladies."

Brian leans back in his chair and pats his obviously fit torso, grinning. Maxine has walked through campus with him and has seen how the students respond to him. She has no doubt he is the object of many coed fantasies, both female and male. She wonders if he has any idea.

"Are there any deadly sins involved?" Brian leans forward in anticipation of something juicy.

Maxine laughs. "I'm pretty sure I worked my way through all of them last weekend." Her smile fades and she fidgets with her flatware, liberating the knife and fork from the rolled paper napkin and lining them up on top of it. This is going to be harder than she thought.

"Maxine." She glances up and sees concern, compassion and not a hint of judgment. "What's wrong?"

The waiter wordlessly clears the leftovers and leaves the check. Brian reaches across the table and squeezes both of Maxine's hands.

"I'm so sorry you had to go through that. It must have been awful." His eyes are wet.

"Nothing really happened to me. At least not... what she went through." Maxine pulls her hands away and reaches for the check. Brian watches her fumble in her purse for her wallet.

"Max, stop. Look at me." She stops and looks up. "What happened may have been different for you, but it was terrifying and violent and traumatic just the same. Just let yourself sit with that for a minute, okay?"

Maxine nods. If she were someone who cried, she'd be a puddle right now. After yesterday's just-the-facts-ma'am police interview (no matter how hot Detective what's-his-name was) and Michael's incredulity, this validation that she had a horrible experience is an intense release. So she does what she always does: she bursts out laughing. For some reason this doesn't seem to surprise Brian.

"I'm sorry, it's just so crazy, isn't it? What was I thinking? I mean, what have I done?" She giggles a little more, and then quiets.

Now Brian's brow furrows in confusion. "You did something that took so much courage, putting yourself in harm's way for a little girl you didn't even know, but you seem to think you've done something wrong. Maxine, what are you really struggling with here?"

Maxine stares for a long time at her hands. There is not a trace of laughter in her eyes as she looks at Father Brian and whispers, "What if I was wrong?"

Anthony Scialfa has been sitting in a small, barren room of the Kirkland Police Station for more than forty-five minutes. On the other side of a large pane of one-way glass, an attractive woman in her late forties with long dark hair asks Chloe a series of banal, seemingly irrelevant questions. Anthony tuned out almost immediately, but two police officers in plain clothes listen intently. One is a tall man and the other is a woman. They spoke with Anthony and Sophie yesterday afternoon at their house, and then with Anthony earlier this morning. Detectives Hancock and Laird, he thinks. They told him that a forensic psychologist would interview Chloe and that the interview would be recorded. Anthony could stay and watch, or he could wait in the lounge.

To look at Anthony sitting there, you'd think he was waiting for a buddy to get off work so they could go for a beer. But he's pretty sure his head will explode if this woman, Dr. Webster, doesn't finish up and bring him his daughter in the next five minutes. Sophie would have demanded to be in the room with Chloe, and initially he was relieved she had been too tired to come with them to the station. Now he wonders if he should have put up more of a fight himself. He's no psychologist, but he can't see how this is getting them any closer to knowing what actually happened.

The breast cancer was one thing. The prognosis was good and the oncologist had been optimistic about Sophie's odds for a full recovery. The mere existence of a team of specialists with a solid treatment plan had been extremely reassuring. He felt he had done an okay job of hiding his darkest fears, and he'd thrown himself into picking up the slack around the house. He had wanted his wife and daughter to feel loved, supported, taken care of and, more than anything, safe. He knew there was nothing he could do to stop Sophie from feeling guilty about missing so much time with Chloe, so he didn't even try. But there was something else going on with her that he couldn't quite figure out. There was a distance, a pulling away from both of them, and he worried that Chloe might have noticed as well. He had kept his focus on the big picture, however, and had truly believed that they would all get through this okay.

This latest violation, however, if there is any truth to it, is not something he can imagine feeling okay about, ever. Unless that woman was mistaken, or demented, unless the forensic psychologist gives them her unconditional guarantee that nothing inappropriate has taken place between Chloe and Deon, he knows their lives have changed in a way that he can never make right. Not for himself, not for Sophie, and certainly not for Chloe.

"Inconclusive." Anthony leans against a wall and watches through the glass as Detective Hancock lifts Chloe as if she is light as a cat so she can put change in a soda machine in the corner of the interview room. The detective waits patiently as she takes a moment to select the right button, and then sets her down gently so she can retrieve her prize. She gives it to him and beams up at him as he opens it and returns it to her little hands. She gulps it greedily.

"I'm sorry, Mr. Scialfa, I know that's not what you want to hear. But children are tricky. I can't lead her one way or the other, and I don't want to scare her any more than she already is. The first visit usually ends up being mostly about building trust, establishing rapport."

"Rapport." Anthony stares at the woman next to him. She is exactly the sort of person with whom you would want to trust your child in this situation. She is professional, forthright, warm and, according to Detective Laird, exceedingly competent. Yet he finds himself longing to wrap his hands around her neck and shake her until she goes limp.

"Kids need to go through the process at their own pace. It's the only way we'll ever get to the truth, but it can be frustrating, I know."

"Frustrating." Anthony is an intelligent, educated man. He is a partner in an architectural firm that specializes in restoring old houses and building new ones in urban areas, focusing on using green materials and choosing quality over square footage. He speaks fluent English and Italian, passable Spanish and more French than his wife realizes. At this moment, however, he is incapable of uttering more than one word at a time.

"We'll meet again in a couple of days. You can arrange a time with the detectives. In the meantime, it's important that you don't try to make her talk. If she volunteers information, that's great. Write down her exact words and call one of the detectives."

Anthony nods and watches as Chloe finishes her pop and the big detective leads her out of the room. She looks like the same little girl she was a week ago, yet everything has changed. Even if it turns out that nothing happened with Deon, the mere fact that Chloe has been in a police station talking with a forensic psychologist feels like a failure on his part.

In the hallway, Anthony rounds a corner and sees Detective Hancock leading Chloe towards him. When she sees Anthony, she runs to him. He scoops her up and buries his face in her hair. She wraps her arms and legs around him tightly, and all is right with his world, for now.

Detective Hancock smiles sympathetically. Anthony wants to punch the big cop so that he'll hit him back and make his pain physical. Instead, he listens and nods as the detective says something about calling for an appointment. Then he turns and takes Chloe out of the station, wondering how to tell Sophie that they have learned absolutely nothing.

When Chloe gets home from the police station, her mom kneels in front of her and hugs her for what feels like forever. Her dad says she was a brave little girl, then clears his throat and disappears into the kitchen. Her mom pulls away, tucks Chloe's dark hair behind her ears and says, "C'est vrai?" Chloe nods, because she figures it is more or less true that she was brave. She was nervous but she didn't cry or anything. Her mom has dark circles under her eyes and Chloe asks her if she feels sicker, but her mom shakes her head and says she's fine, then smiles and hugs Chloe some more and asks her to run up to her room for a minute so she can talk to Daddy.

Chloe listens by her bedroom door but can hear only a muffled conversation, her mom's voice louder than her dad's. Then the front door closes, a little harder than normal. After a few minutes of silence, her mom calls, "Chloe? It's time for lunch, ma précieuse."

Chloe's mom has made egg salad, one of her favorites, and they take their sandwiches and lemonade out to the backyard and have a picnic, big blanket and all. Her mom remembers some of the games they used to play, like trying to see different shapes in the clouds and seeing who can point out the most butterflies. Her mother sees fantastical shapes in the clouds, like lovers kissing and ballerinas dancing. Chloe mostly sees bunnies and cars. Chloe almost always spies more butterflies than her mom, though. Her mom says she has an eagle eye. They haven't done this since last summer. When her mom doesn't eat much and has to lie back for a minute before they bring everything back inside, Chloe pretends not to notice.

Usually, this summer anyway, after lunch she would go to the park or the pool or the zoo with Uncle Deon, or just to his house. Today her mom says Deon is going to be busy for a while.

"You're stuck with boring old Mommy." She puts a hand to her forehead dramatically. "Quel dommage, non?" Chloe giggles.

Chloe watches a movie on DVD with her mom curled up on the sofa next to her, sleeping. She's seen this movie about a hundred times, but she doesn't mind. She tries to be still, and she checks every now and then to make sure the light blanket covering her mom is still rising and falling over her tummy.

During his lunch hour, Michael efficiently completes preparations for Maxine's birthday tomorrow. He confirms their dinner reservations, which were a feat to secure on a summer Saturday, regardless of his carefully cultivated relationship with the maître d', Vicente. He hops into his car and drives downtown to pick up the ivory cashmere sweater, exquisitely wrapped by an obsequious store clerk, then stops at an upscale market on the way back to his office for a birthday card and for tomorrow's breakfast: sesame bagels, cream cheese, smoked salmon, a red onion, capers and fresh squeezed orange juice.

At work, he stores the food in the office refrigerator, the bag labeled "Dr. Silver" in bold red marker. On his computer monitor, he affixes a note reminding him to take everything with him when he leaves for the day. He leans back in his chair and stares out the window, wondering if Maxine will even feel like celebrating, given the circumstances. It's not as though he's throwing a surprise party, he figures, and they have to eat, so he decides to go ahead with his plans and try to be sensitive to her mood throughout the day.

The phrase "press charges" has been intruding on Michael's thoughts all morning. He taps a few keys on his computer and pulls up the file for his next client, but his mind returns to Maxine. He finds it surprisingly easy to picture her kicking a grown man to the ground. Maxine has always been quick to anger. In fact, her mercurial nature is a trait he finds strangely appealing and challenging. Still, he wonders what in the world made her follow the man and girl into the house. Why would she suspect sexual abuse? It seems a rather morbid conclusion. A notion Michael's subconscious resists slowly takes shape. When it finally bursts forth, fully formed, he closes his eyes and rests his head in his hands. *Was Maxine molested as a child?*

CHAPTER THREE

Chloe loves Saturdays, especially during the summer. Saturdays mean getting up early and going to the farmers market with her parents, then making breakfast with whatever yummy fruits, veggies and other treasures they bring home. Mom buys bunches of flowers and scatters them around the house in vases and pitchers. Later, their bellies full and the house smelling of lavender and lilies, Dad reads the newspaper and Mom curls up with a book, while Chloe draws or reads her own books.

This summer her mom has been too sick for the market, and Chloe goes with just her dad. Sometimes they don't buy the right things and her mom gets mad, and sometimes her mom's too tired to eat breakfast at all. Lately, though, she seems less cross, and she eats with them more often, too.

In the afternoon Chloe's father takes her to the park or the pool, or if the weather is bad they'll see a movie or go to the library. This has always been their time alone together. The only difference now is that, on the ride home, he asks if she has any question about her mom's sickness.

Chloe has lots of questions. *Will Mommy's hair grow back? What if her other breast gets sick? Will they be able to go on vacation this summer?* And, of course, *Is Mommy going to die?* But she never asks those questions. She just asks if Mommy is getting better. And her father always says yes.

Sometimes before dinner, Chloe goes down the street to play with her best friend Haley, or Haley comes over to her house. Sometimes she plays by herself in her room or helps her mom in the garden. Either way, she knows both her mom and dad are home. Even when her mom is at her sickest and Chloe can hear her throwing up or her dad says she's sleeping, they are both there. This is when Chloe feels most like other kids. Safe.

This Saturday morning, after Chloe dresses and goes down into the kitchen, she can hardly believe her eyes. Her father gulps the last of his coffee and plucks his car keys from a basket on the counter while her mother pulls sunglasses out of her purse, adjusts the scarf covering her patchy tufts of hair, and then claps her hands and chirps, "Okay then. Allons-y!"

Her dad opens the door from the kitchen to the garage. Her mom sashays out and settles delicately into the front passenger seat, checking her reflection in the visor mirror. Her father grins. "You heard the lady. Let's go!"

Chloe devours her omelet hungrily. She wishes they could have stayed longer at the market, but her dad kept glancing at her mom and hurrying them all from one stall to the next. They bought fresh eggs, mushrooms, goat cheese, figs, peaches, some herbs they didn't have in their own garden, arugula and bunches of lavender, and then her dad announced, "Mission accomplished! Let's go home and eat!" and they headed back to the car. Chloe wanted to look at the pastries and berries and jams, but she didn't say anything. She just dragged her feet on the way to the parking lot until her father turned around and said, "Shake a leg, Chloe."

Now, watching her mom pick at her own breakfast, Chloe sees how tired she is and feels bad for dawdling. She wants her mom to get better more than anything in the world, and tells herself for the hundredth time that she will do whatever it takes to help her.

Maxine dresses carefully for dinner. She knows Michael will want to see her in her new sweater, but she's not sure how to complete the outfit. She could wear a short, flirty skirt to show off her legs, but she doesn't want to look slutty. She considers a long, black, silk skirt but worries it may be too dressy. The restaurant is elegant, yet their community is surprisingly casual when it comes to dining out. Michael, however, is not. Lately she finds herself struggling more than ever to look appropriate. After some deliberation, she picks a pair of sleek black linen trousers and mid-heeled black mules.

Selecting jewelry is easier; she chooses from the pieces Michael has given her over the years. She limits herself to one striking item, such as the diamond, pearl and white gold pendant she fastens around her neck tonight, and then complements it with a simple white-gold bracelet and small white-gold hoop earrings. It's conservative for her taste, but Maxine knows Michael loves seeing her dressed this way.

Michael is always thoughtful on birthdays, and today Maxine is having fun, without feeling too pressured to have fun. She enjoys both Michael's attention and the chance to temporarily leave behind the events of the last couple of days. She has a vague awareness that she is being handled, yet so expertly that she doesn't really mind.

Sitting at her vanity, Maxine applies makeup sparingly. She has just finished smoothing her hair into a low ponytail when Michael emerges from the closet, looking effortlessly stylish in a beige linen suit, relaxed white dress shirt and shoes that can only be described as casually dressy. Maxine muses that he is the only man she has ever dated who wears outfits rather than mere clothes.

Michael motions for Maxine to stand. She rises and twirls slowly, then strikes a seductive pose. He nods appreciatively, then his brow furrows.

"Hair down, maybe?"

Maxine shrugs and removes the clasp, shaking her hair loose over her shoulders.

Michael smiles as he approaches her. He strokes her hair, grazing her cashmere-covered breast in the process. "Perfect. I don't deserve you."

Anthony turns over three steaks in a frying pan, checks his watch and adjusts the heat on the gas burner. He takes a sip of wine and glances at Chloe setting the kitchen table and Sophie sorting the mail. His girls had a good day, and he is pleased. Suddenly he is struck by the absurdity of that. When did one good day become the anomaly?

He smiles at Chloe as he hands her the salad to put on the table, then turns and shuts off the oven. He removes three foil wrapped baked potatoes with an oven mitt and sets them on the counter, then turns off the burner and moves the steaks to a plate, covering them with foil.

"Something here from your father," Sophie announces. "Little early this year, isn't it?"

"Well let's have a look at it then. It must be important." Anthony reaches out a hand and taps his foot impatiently.

"No, Daddy, you have to wait for your birthday!" Chloe jumps between Anthony and Sophie and grabs Anthony's hand with both of hers to ensure no letter exchange takes place. He smacks his forehead with his free hand.

"That's right! It's a good thing you were here or I would have completely forgotten." He pulls Chloe to him and tickles her. She giggles. Anthony sees Sophie grin and roll her eyes at his teasing, at these predictable annual theatrics. She waves the letter at Anthony and props it in a prominent position on the kitchen counter.

"Come and get it, ladies." Anthony plops a juicy steak and a baked potato on each plate, then takes his own plate and wine glass and joins his family at the table. Sophie dishes out salad, then unwraps and cuts open Chloe's potato, dropping a generous dollop of butter in the steamy center. She pours herself a splash of wine and holds it aloft, as does Anthony. Chloe lifts her glass of milk.

Sophie chirps, "Bon appétit!"

Anthony replies, "Buon appetito!"

As Anthony and Sophie start to sip their wine, Chloe chimes in, "¡Buen provecho!" Anthony and Sophie turn to stare at her.

She shrugs. "Uncle Deon taught it to me. He says Spanish will be way bigger than French or Italian pretty soon. Spanish and Chinese." Chloe takes a swig of milk and tucks into her buttery potato.

Anthony drains his wine, sets down the glass and stares at his food. When he glances at Sophie, her face is a mask of passivity. She delicately stabs her steak, dissecting it into small pieces that she does not eat.

Anthony sees Chloe look at him, at Sophie. Chloe stops chewing, and with a mouthful of potato asks, "What?"

On the short drive home, Michael is randy as hell. For one thing, this was the slam dunk of all birthdays and he's pleased with himself. The day was fun and low key. Maxine loved her present. Dinner was perfect, beginning with Vicente bowing slightly and murmuring, "Good evening, Mr. Silver. Your table is ready."

There was a brief moment of tension when Maxine announced her plans to fly home when Astrid, her closest friend since childhood, gave birth to her baby. Astrid was due any day now, and Michael's suggestion that this might not be the best time to leave town was greeted with a surprised silence. Fortunately, he realized this was not the time to discuss it, and quickly changed the subject.

He couldn't argue with Maxine when she looked this sexy, anyway. In the soft light of the restaurant, he

Soft Landing

could see she was wearing a black bra under the pale tank, even though he had made certain it was quality two-ply cashmere. He found this just a bit trashy and therefore a huge turn on. He knew it wasn't contrived on her part; she most likely put on a black bra this morning and didn't think to change it when she was dressing for dinner.

Now he's getting a hard on wondering what is under those black pants. On the way out of the restaurant, after a warm, "We hope to see you again soon, Mr. Silver!" from Vicente, Michael walked behind Maxine for a moment to appreciate her ass. He had noted the absence of pantylines and hopes this means she is wearing a thong.

By the time he pulls into the driveway his linen pants are visibly tented. As the garage door inches upward, he touches Maxine's cheek and murmurs, "I love you, baby. God, you're beautiful."

Maxine grins and replies, "I love you too, and you can stop finessing me now. I'm pretty much a sure thing." She proves this by resting her hand on his crotch. He hits the gas and the car lurches forward into the garage. Maxine takes off her seat belt, and as Michael turns off the ignition and punches the garage door remote, she fiddles with his pants and liberates his erection. She leans over and teases him with her mouth until he groans. She sits up and licks his lips lightly, then hops out of the car and beckons him to follow her before disappearing into the house.

Michael hurries after her, entering through the open door, prick first. Maxine stands at the kitchen sink, filling a glass with water. He comes up behind her and fills his hands with her breasts. She turns and hands him the water, then walks away, pulling her tank over her head and tossing it on a dining room chair. In the living room, she kicks off her shoes. He follows her up the stairs as she unbuttons and unzips her pants, then she stops and turns at the door to their bedroom and lets her pants fall around her feet. She turns her back to Michael and bends over to pick them up. Michael smiles at the sight of her thong and takes a gulp of water.

Michael knew he would fuck Maxine the first time he saw her. He and the partners in his first practice in Chicago were investing in a new computer network and Maxine pitched her consulting services. She was knowledgeable and confident but, unlike her competitors, not at all deferential. In fact, she was a bit arrogant and he suspected she believed they would be lucky to have her. Michael fought his partners, particularly the women, to hire her.

Fortunately, the project was a success, and once it was completed, he asked her out. They clicked, but she put him through an excruciating six weeks of dating before she let him into her bed. It was worth it.

Now, after three years, sex with Maxine is as exciting to Michael as it was then. He doesn't have any idea how many sexual partners she's had, nor does he particularly want to, but she's clearly experienced and enjoys being in control. Of course, he's had his share of women and has no doubts about his own skills in the bedroom. Yet something about Maxine's performances keeps him guessing, wondering what to expect next.

Michael stares at her astride him, her long blond hair allowing him glimpses of her breasts as she rocks back and forth, eyes closed. He reaches up and pushes her hair behind her shoulders, pinching her nipples. Her eyes open and she moans and gives him a little nod to let him know she's about to have her second orgasm and now would be a good time for him to finish up. He wants them to look at each other as they come together, but she always closes her eyes at the last minute.

One recent development is that Maxine no longer cuddles after sex. As a psychologist, Michael knows he should probably explore the significance of this change in behavior. As a man, he's mostly relieved. Tonight, she rolls off him and they lie on their backs holding hands until Maxine's breathing slows. Then she pads into the bathroom, pees, brushes her teeth and is back in bed, curled up with her back to him, within five minutes. Michael decides to talk to her about it some other time. He turns on his side and puts a hand on her shoulder and whispers, "Happy birthday, baby."

Maxine squeezes his hand and mumbles, "Mmmm. You too."

Chloe isn't sleepy. Her body is tired from a busy day and her brain is tired from worrying about what to say and what not to say. On their ride home from the pool, her dad asked her again if she wanted to talk about Mommy. This time, instead of asking a question, Chloe thought about it for a moment and declared, "I think Mommy is getting better." Her dad grinned and said, "Kinda looks that way, doesn't it?"

Then he said that she could talk to Mommy or Daddy about anything. He said, "If there's anything you want to tell us, or ask us, even if it's about Mommy's sickness, or Uncle Deon or anything else, it's okay. Okay?"

She said okay and that was that. Then at dinner when she told them what Uncle Deon said about Spanish and Chinese they both got all weird and quiet for a minute. She had just blurted it out without thinking but she knew right away it was wrong. They tried to pretend it was fine and act normal after that, but for the rest of dinner, Chloe pictured today as a balloon filled with good things. Then someone stuck a pin in it and all the good whooshed out. Maybe one day could hold only so much good and then it had to pop. She just wished she hadn't been the one with the pin.

When Daddy put her to bed he talked to her about their heritage and how he was a first-generation Italian American and Mommy was born in France and how they were proud of that and wanted Chloe to be proud, too. He said she could take up any language she liked, but maybe Uncle Deon shouldn't be the only one to help her pick which one. When he said "Uncle Deon" his voice sounded funny and he looked away for a second before tucking her in and kissing her good night. Now, lying in bed, tired but not sleepy, she reminds herself to be careful not to pop the balloon again.

CHAPTER FOUR

Anthony sips coffee early Sunday morning while Sophie and Chloe sleep. He rarely has a moment to himself these last few months, and it has become his habit to rise and clear his head before another day overtakes him. Today, however, his head is a junkyard of rusty, dismembered car parts waiting to be processed, and he feels a sense of defeat settling in even before the sun is completely up.

His eye is drawn to the letter from his father, propped on the counter by Sophie last night. He stares at it and feels a twinge of irritation that his father has been so inaccessible of late. Last year, months before Sophie became ill, Anthony was unusually busy at work and by the time he got home, with the three-hour time difference, it was too late too call his father in New York. He had sent him an answering machine for his last birthday so they could at least trade messages, but his father complained it was too complicated to set up and didn't work properly. Since Sophie's illness, his dad has made a point of checking in, but his calls stopped abruptly a week or so ago.

Anthony has left repeated messages and even called during the day, but hasn't made contact.

It occurs to Anthony that he needn't talk to his father to communicate with him. He refills his coffee cup and heads into the downstairs bedroom, which they use as an office. From the top shelf in the closet, he retrieves a shoebox and sets it on the desk, brushing a year's worth of dust from the cover. He lifts the lid and unfolds the top letter, written almost a year ago, and smiles at the scrawling, familiar handwriting.

Anthony's father has written him a letter on each birthday since he was born. When he learned to read, he caught up on the first several years, which were mostly stories and observations about his emerging personality. Over time they became more of a user's manual on how to be a good boy and, later, how to be a good man. Most birthdays he looked forward to reading them.

Anthony,   *July 10, 2006*

In the summer of '83 I was bumped up to foreman of a big new office building project in Manhattan. I was proud and determined to impress my bosses with my commitment to the job. And honestly, I didn't mind feeling like a man in charge for a change. (Your mother ran a tight ship, God rest her soul.) I missed a lot of dinners and worked a lot of weekends, and your poor mother had her hands full with you two. And then your sister got sick. I remember how I felt knowing I could never get that time back.

Soft Landing

As a man you work to feed your family and keep a roof over your heads. If your work keeps you from sharing meals with your family or spending time with them in your home, it may be wise to ask yourself why.

Is your job more important than your family? I know it is not to you. Are you struggling to earn a comfortable living? I believe you are doing well financially. Do you find more satisfaction in your professional life than your personal life? If you are doing work that you love, it is almost inevitable, because often the roles of husband and father seem thankless. You are fortunate to have found a career that brings you joy, and I am proud of you, as your mother was. But a man who chooses to marry and have a family must remember how precious that family is and that they are always his first priority. I know there are times at work when you are busier than others, but please don't make a habit of giving the best of yourself to your job. Save that for your beautiful wife and daughter. You will never regret it.

Tu Padre

Anthony refolds this letter carefully, recalling his indignation at the gentle rebuke. At the time, he was a bit full of himself in his career and didn't want his father, or his wife, giving him grief about how much time he spent working. Becoming a partner at his firm was a big step for him. The long hours were temporary, he had told himself. Of course, he had no idea how prophetic his father's words would prove. He makes the connection for the first time, and the hairs on his arms stand on end. Hearing noises from the kitchen, he replaces the letter and covers the box, but does not return it to the closet.

Maxine has a hangover, and each time she bends to pick up an item from last night's trail of clothing, her head pounds. Michael rarely overindulges and therefore sprang out of bed early to go for a jog before the day became too warm. In the closet, she carefully folds the cashmere tank and adds it to a neat stack of clothing reserved for special occasions, mostly gifts from Michael.

She's sipping coffee and trying to decide whether to bother showering or just curl up and read when the phone rings. She knows before picking up the receiver that it's Astrid, and that she's had her baby.

"Boy or girl?" Maxine whispers into the phone.

"A girl, Max, and she is the most perfect thing I have ever seen." Astrid's voice catches. She takes a deep breath and continues, "Star Charity Maxine Campbell, born 4:52 this morning, a seven pound, one ounce, twenty one inch bundle of pure joy. Isn't that right my sweet precious angel?"

Maxine hears a gurgle from the angel and, unbidden, a sound that is half laugh, half sob escapes her own lips. She takes a few deep breaths before asking, "So everything went okay?"

"It was amazing. I wish you could have been here. She was born at home, of course, and our midwife was fantastic. I swear she massaged my perineum for two hours so I wouldn't tear." Maxine has no idea what this is and doesn't want to. "The whole thing hurt like a motherfucker, don't get me wrong, but when I heard her cry and John laid her on my breast I felt so... whole."

Maxine giggles. Astrid doesn't miss a beat. "There's an open round trip ticket waiting for you. John's emailing the itinerary to you right now. Can you come tomorrow?"

"Of course I can. Astrid?"

"What, sweetie?"

"Congratulations. I love you."

"I know. I love you too. Now get your ass on a plane and come meet your goddaughter."

Chloe picks at her fingernails. "But I already talked to her, like, forever."

"You did, and you did really great. She just has a few more questions to ask you." Chloe looks at her dad and frowns.

"Then why didn't she ask them when I was there?" This seems like a perfectly good question to Chloe.

Her dad shrugs. "Maybe she didn't want you to get too tired. She doesn't know what a tough little bug you are." He grins and ruffles Chloe's hair. "I'm sorry, but it's important, Chloe. It's important that you talk to her and that you're completely honest with her. Okay?"

Chloe looks away. "Whatever. Will the big policeman be there again? He was nice."

Anthony sighs. "I suppose he will be."

Chloe nods, wondering what she can get out of the deal. "Can I have a soda afterwards?"

Chloe doesn't like Sundays as much as Saturdays because there is no farmers market, but they're still better than weekdays because both her parents are home. This one isn't going so great, though. She heard her parents arguing in their bedroom when she woke up. Then her dad told her she had to talk to that lady again. The last time she didn't know what to say and it all seemed stupid, but then her mom was so proud of her and started to feel so much better afterwards, Chloe decided it was worth it. She just hopes she can get it right again. She stays in her room most of the afternoon worrying about it.

On Sundays, Chloe doesn't spend as much time with her parents because they're busy with their Sunday chores. Her mom does laundry and cleans as best she can while her dad works in the yard and tries to fix things around the house. Her mom always jokes that if Chloe wants someone handy around, she'd be far better off marrying an electrician or a plumber than an architect. Chloe doesn't tell her mom this, but she doesn't ever want to get married. For one thing, the boys she knows are gross. And even if she does like boys someday, as her mom promises she will, she'll be way too busy working and traveling and shopping to have time for a husband and family.

She knows her mom loves her and her dad, but sometimes she looks so sad Chloe thinks maybe she wishes she had a different life. Chloe doesn't blame her, really; she could still be living in France. Chloe has been to visit her mom's family a few times, and she can't imagine ever wanting to leave. In her mind, France is the most fantastic place in the world, where dogs are allowed in restaurants, there are street markets everywhere and all the women look like movie stars. Why would anyone leave all of that behind to be here?

Maxine tosses another bra — black, Michael notices — into her suitcase and continues shouting, "Maybe I wouldn't be defensive if you'd stop treating me like a criminal. For Christ's sake, Michael, I'm not out on bail!"

Michael broached the subject tactfully so that Maxine would hear his concern and not become defensive, but she was resistant the moment he opened his mouth and progressed rapidly from unreasonable to completely irrational. He knows there's no point in pursuing this argument, that her mind was made up weeks ago, but he can't seem to let it go. He has no problem with her wanting to see Astrid and the baby, although usually her visits to Bozeman leave her drained and moody. He just can't help but question the timing.

"Of course you're not a criminal. I just don't understand why we can't get past this... situation before you go. There'll be plenty of time to see the baby."

Maxine turns and stares at him coldly, then smiles. She disappears from the bedroom and Michael hears her footsteps quickly descending the stairs. Exasperated and confused, he yells after her, "What the hell are you doing now?"

A few minutes pass, during which time Michael wonders why he bothers trying to help her. Then Maxine reappears waving a business card in one hand and a phone in the other. She peers at the card and dials a number, and then holds the phone to her ear with an exaggerated air of anticipation, her eyes fixed on Michael.

"Detective Hancock? Hi, this is Maxine Reise, from the other day with the little girl?" Michael recognizes the same deferential tone that surprised him before. A low laugh from Maxine, then, "Right, the kick boxer. I hate to bother you, but my best friend just had a baby and I was planning to fly to Bozeman to see her. I wanted to make sure you wouldn't think I was fleeing the jurisdiction or anything." Michael rolls his eyes. Maxine chuckles again and continues, "No sir, no more than a few days." A pause. "Fiancé. We're not married yet. But sure, you can reach me through him or you could call me on my cell..."

Michael turns and retreats to the office down the hall. He sinks into a leather club chair and tries to find some positive in the situation by hoping a few days away will do Maxine some good. Their relationship might also benefit from a short break.

He hopes Astrid will be too preoccupied with the baby to have her usual influence on Maxine. The last time Maxine spent time with Astrid, she came home with plans for an elaborate vegetable and herb garden. The time before that she wanted to install a rain barrel to avoid wasting water in the garden. Before they moved here, he vividly remembers her insistence after a trip to Bozeman that they consider buying a hybrid car. He doesn't have a problem with any of these ideas in theory; he just feels he and Maxine need to prioritize their time and money more appropriately.

Michael is aware that Astrid doesn't like him. He doesn't care what she thinks of him, of course, but he's sorry that Maxine is caught in the middle and wishes Astrid wouldn't put her in such a position.

Then there are Maxine's mother, Barb, and sister, Lucy. Widowed when Maxine was nine and Lucy was just a baby, remarried within two years and divorced around the time Lucy left for college, Barb is actively seeking husband number three. What intrigues Michael is the effect Barb's presence has on Maxine. Around her mother, Maxine becomes tense and fractious, like a surly teenager. Michael has certainly seen worse relationships between mothers and daughters, but Maxine has a great deal of anger toward her mother and he wishes he knew why. Barb has always seemed intelligent, charming and witty to him, but Maxine's foul temper can linger for days after seeing her.

Maxine's relationship with her sister, on the other hand, is practically nonexistent. The age gap might explain the emotional distance between them, but Michael doesn't believe that Maxine isn't interested in her sister. Lucy clearly looks up to Maxine, but when they are together, Maxine is awkward and overly solicitous, as if she wants to make a connection but something is in the way.

Michael has no siblings and has a perfectly cordial relationship with his parents, but he spends his days working with troubled children and is fascinated by family dynamics and how utterly dysfunctional they can become. Maxine never talks about her family, not even about her dead father. He wonders if she will ever open up to him about her childhood.

"You'll be relieved to know that I'm authorized to travel. Within reason, of course. Satisfied?"

Startled, Michael jumps slightly and looks up at Maxine standing in the doorway. She appears pleased with herself but somewhat conciliatory. Never a dull moment. Michael smiles. Maybe a quick makeup fuck.

Chloe has just gone to bed and Sophie is curled up with a book at the other end of the sofa, but Anthony feels as if there is a giant spring under his ass. He fights the urge to jump up and do something, anything. He's anxious about tomorrow, but there's something else gnawing at him.

"I haven't been able to get a hold of my father."

Sophie looks up. "When did you talk to him last?"

"Maybe a week or so ago. But I've left messages and tried him during the day, and still, nothing."

Sophie shakes her head. "You know he never gets his messages." Her brow furrows and then she grins. "Maybe he's found himself a lady friend."

Anthony laughs, surprised by the unfamiliarity of the sound. "He wouldn't. You know he thinks my mom still talks to him and watches his every move, — "

"God rest her soul," Sophie chimes in, smiling. "Call him now. It's not even midnight there."

"Holy Christ, he'd have a heart attack. No, I'll try him first thing in the morning."

The giant spring prevails and Anthony rises. "I'm gonna clean up my desk a bit." He leans over and kisses Sophie. He smoothes her patches of hair, then presses his lips to the top of her head. She takes his hand and holds it a little tighter and for a little longer than she used to.

"Try not to worry, Anthony. I'm sure he's fine."

Soft Landing

Anthony,   July 10, 1964

Welcome, my beautiful son! How blessed we are at this moment. Your mother fought like a lioness to bring you into this world, and I swear on a stack of Bibles it took three nurses to pull you from her arms so they could wash you and count your fingers and toes. And you are perfect! If you could see your mother smile every time she looks at you.

You are a first generation American, the first in our family to be born a citizen of the United States of America. Someday you will understand what this means, and I know you will be as proud as we are of you right now. And may you always be proud of your Italian heritage, for your ancestors have built much of New York, this amazing city that is our home.

We will always love you with all our hearts,
Tu Padre

Anthony smiles at the thought of anyone attempting to take something from his mother that she wasn't prepared to let go. He skips ahead a few letters, surprised by how interesting he still finds them.

Anthony,   July 10, 1968

How quickly you've grown! Your mother says you must have an old soul because sometimes you look like the weight of the world is on your little shoulders, but I think you are just smarter and more thoughtful than the other boys. Your kind nature and quick sense of humor are sure to win you many friends in our new neighborhood, mark my words. And how you adore your sister! You keep surprising us with how gentle and protective you are with her, when we feared you might be jealous. She is lucky to have such a loving big brother and I think she knows it, the way she follows you everywhere.

You must be so excited about starting school next year. When I started kindergarten I didn't speak a word of English, but young minds soak up knowledge faster than you'd imagine, and I can't wait to see what catches your interest as you begin to make your way in the world.

We are so proud of you. I truly hope that one day you have a child, not only because we want to be grandparents (which we do!), but also because only then will you really understand how much we love you.

Tu Padre

Anthony doesn't remember being four, of course, but photos he has seen depict a slight, serious boy who does, indeed, look as if he is carrying the weight of the world. In almost every picture, his sister gazes up at him adoringly. Anthony has tears in his eyes as he folds this letter and tucks it between the others. He hears Sophie making her way slowly up the stairs, and he turns out the light as he leaves the room with its box full of ghosts, deciding he's had enough of the past for tonight.

CHAPTER FIVE

Michael drives Maxine to the airport first thing in the morning. Maxine figures he feels guilty about last night's argument and grateful for the spectacular blowjob she gave him afterwards. She suspects he also wants to make sure she doesn't get too drunk to get on the plane. She's already buzzed from the Bailey's she had in her morning coffee.

At the airport bar, Maxine flags down the bartender. "A Bloody Mary, please. A double would be great." The bartender looks at her as if she's nuts and informs her that a double will cost nine dollars. Maxine replies, "Well okay then." Michael pays the bartender when he returns with the drink. Maxine takes a gulp and ends up with a mouthful of straight vodka since she neglected to stir it. Her eyes tear up and she stirs the Bloody Mary with shaking hands.

Michael says, "Maybe you should consider seeing someone about this flying phobia. It seems to be getting worse."

Maxine takes another gulp. "You see, that's where

you're confused. I don't think it's irrational to be afraid of flying. It's people like you who are crazy." She's a bit slurry but dead serious.

Michael watches Maxine take several swigs of her drink, and then he sighs. "I'm sorry about last night, baby. I know this is hard for you. I hope Astrid appreciates what a good friend you are." He tucks her hair behind her ear and strokes her back as she finishes her drink.

Waiting in line at the security checkpoint, Maxine listens closely to Michael's instructions. "Give my best to Astrid and John. And to your mom, of course. Try not to let her drive you crazy." As they hug and kiss good-bye, she thinks about how he always comes through for her in the end, and she promises herself to remember this and try not to be so prickly when she gets home. She jots it down in her journal when she gets on the plane. Once the plane has taken off safely, she even mentions it to the woman sitting next to her, despite Michael's warning to resist the urge to chat with her seatmate because yes, they probably will be able to tell she is drunk.

As she settles in for the short flight, Maxine has the sensation of losing definition, as if little bits of her are coming loose and scattering in different directions, a dried out sandcastle eroded by the wind. Being inebriated is part of it, but there's more. She feels unmoored, drifting from apprehension to anticipation and back again, as if this journey is about more than just meeting Astrid's baby.

Maxine is searching through Astrid's closet for something to wear. Astrid is a little taller and thinner than Maxine, and all of her clothes are either loose and flowing and too long, or fitted and too tight. Maxine is getting frantic, and she's not too happy with the way Astrid is sitting on her bed, watching her with a little smile.

"Would it kill you to help me?" Maxine snaps, pulling off a gauzy peasant blouse that makes her look huge, even though she's not. Astrid's parents are hippies and don't believe in air conditioning, and it's about 104 degrees in Astrid's bedroom, which is in the attic. Maxine's sweating like crazy, and this makes it almost impossible to wiggle out of a pair of too-tight Levi's. She feels her panic building.

"Max, it's a pot party, not a prom. You looked fine in your own clothes. Believe me, nobody will give a shit what you're wearing. Neither will you five minutes after you get there." Astrid continues brushing her hair and looking as if she's enjoying her own little private joke.

Astrid's closet is impossibly huge and stuffed with clothes, and it seems the more Maxine tries on, the more new clothes appear that weren't there before. She's sure she could achieve the appropriately earthy, natural look if only she had more time. But they're running late, and since it takes Astrid about five minutes to look perfect for any occasion, she isn't likely to take pity on Maxine right now.

Maxine mutters, "I don't want to embarrass you by looking too preppy in front of your granola friends. God forbid."

"God forbid you should relax and be yourself for a change."

That stings, but the best Maxine can come up with is a weak "Fuck you." She's standing in her underwear in front of the closet, pulling things out and rejecting them, flinging them in a growing pile on the floor. Her head is pounding and her throat is dry, and she has to pee like crazy, but she knows she's running out of time. Suddenly, these clothes don't look like Astrid's anymore; they are crazy colors and fabrics, and Maxine realizes Astrid is trying to trick her. "Where are your real clothes?" Maxine demands, whirling around.

"Fuck me? Where are my real clothes?" Astrid parrots sarcastically, getting up off the bed and coming towards Max, holding the hairbrush menacingly by her side. Suddenly Maxine feels stoned, and very paranoid, and tries to remember if they did a little pre-heating for the party. She's terrified, and as she moves toward the stairs to get away from Astrid, she realizes she's wearing only her underwear, but there is no time to look for her jeans and T-shirt in this mess of clothes. She reaches the top of the stairs and turns to look at Astrid, and suddenly the room is much longer and Astrid appears small and sad and far away, and not at all threatening. She says softly, "Where are you going?" Maxine trips on the top step and feels herself falling. She hits with a jolt, continues falling, then another jolt, and another...

Maxine wakes with a start to the pilot announcing they are encountering some turbulence, and would everyone please remain seated with their seatbelts fastened until they have landed in approximately sixteen minutes. She is relieved to see that she is fully clothed, but the crushing headache from the dream is a reality and she needs to pee. Maxine hates flying hangovers. Irritably, she wishes Michael were a psychiatrist so he could prescribe her Valium.

Despite Maxine's certainty that the landing gear has not been deployed, the plane touches down smoothly and taxis to the gate. Her hangover kicks in with full force now.

Soft Landing

Sweat rolls down her back and her stomach churns. She calculates that she must endure at least thirty minutes of walking, riding in the car and making conversation with her mother before she will be able to lie down. She gathers her carry-on and makes her way down the aisle and into the tiny airport. She spots a restroom and hurries in, squeezing into the first vacant stall. When she's finished peeing, she remains seated with her head between her knees, waiting for the waves of nausea to pass. At the sink, she washes her hands and lets cold water run over her wrists for a minute, then glances in the mirror and winces. She looks like a mannequin of herself, pale and waxy with dark smudges under her eyes. As she leaves the restroom, she gropes in her purse for her heavy-duty migraine meds, and swallows two at a water fountain.

She absently hopes her mom doesn't notice what a mess she is as she spots her car at the curbside pickup. Her mom hops out for a quick kiss and hug, then peers at her. "Good Lord, Maxine, you look like hell. What's wrong with you?" Her tone and expression convey both concern and accusation, a combination that has always confused and irritated the hell out of Maxine.

"Got a little headache. Straight home, okay?"

Maxine collapses into the passenger seat and closes her eyes. She wraps her arms around her head, one at the base of her skull and the other on her forehead, viselike, waiting for the painkillers to kick in. She senses her mom studying her for a moment as the engine idles. *Just go already.* Then the car suddenly pulls away from the curb and they're off. Her mom drives like a teenage boy, alternately accelerating and braking abruptly and weaving in and out of lanes. She's not in a hurry; this is just the way she drives. Maxine is grateful for the speed but fears the weaving may become a problem.

A horn blasts behind them as her mom cuts in front of someone. Her mom mutters, "Piss off," then chirps brightly, "I hope you don't mind, but I've got a date tonight. Dr. Cantor — pediatrician, divorced, big house in the hills. We're going to a benefit auction."

Maxine feigns interest, "First date?"

"First date, yes, but not a blind date, thank God. We met at a party. Elaine told me he has a vacation house somewhere, too — North Carolina she thought."

"Wow," Maxine mumbles. She knows her mom doesn't like to talk too much about a prospect that might be worth keeping, for fear of jinxing it. Dr. Cantor must be a catch because she quickly changes the subject.

"How's Michael? And Astrid and the baby? And, oh hell, what's her husband's name?"

Maxine rolls down the window for some fresh air, feeling her stomach turn and her mouth water. "John. Michael's fine. They're all fine. Can't talk now, Mom — makes me nauseous." She leans over with her head between her knees. She just needs to make it another five minutes or so. "Could you maybe drive a little faster?"

"Good Lord, Maxine."

"He isn't really my uncle."

"Oh?" Dr. Webster doesn't really say much. Chloe alternately picks at her fingernails and sneaks glances at Dr. Webster's clothes and shoes. Dr. Webster sits on the floor, cross-legged, while Chloe sits in a small chair at a low table spread with paper and crayons. When they first started, Dr. Webster asked her to draw her family, which she did quickly and easily, since she loves to draw almost as much as her dad does. Dr. Webster asked her about her relationship with her mom and dad, shown on either side of her in the picture. Then she asked, "Where's Uncle Deon in this picture?"

Now Chloe explains, "I mean he's not my real uncle. My mom was a foreign exchange student in high school and she lived with Deon's family. So we always just call him Uncle Deon."

Dr. Webster nods at Chloe but doesn't say anything. Chloe continues, "My mom is French, you know. I mean, she grew up in France and just moved to America to be with my dad. They met in New York when my mom went to college there for a little while. I can't imagine ever wanting to live here instead of France." Chloe thinks this sounds very grown up and sophisticated.

"You don't like living here?"

Chloe shrugs. "It's okay, I guess. But if I were my mom I would have made my dad move there instead."

"How do you think your mom feels about living here?"

Chloe thinks about this carefully. "She's been really sad for a while. You know, since she got sick."

"What about before she was sick? Was she sad then?"

Chloe doesn't really know how to answer this. "Sometimes. She says Americans are obsessed with being happy all the time, but it's okay to be grumpy in France."

Dr. Webster smiles. "What do you think made her sadder when she was sick?"

Chloe thinks this is a pretty stupid question, but as she starts to answer she suddenly feels like she might cry. "Well, she doesn't feel good!" she snaps, and then stops as her voice catches. She blinks hard and keeps blinking until the tightness in the back of her throat goes away.

Dr. Webster nods. "Anything else?"

Chloe picks furiously at her nails. She looks up at Dr. Webster's friendly, concerned face and opens her mouth, but nothing comes out.

"Chloe? What else has been making your mom sad? Other than not feeling well."

Chloe blurts out, "She can't be with me as much as she was before. Some days I hardly even see her!"

Dr. Webster nods. "That must make you feel sad, too, huh?"

Chloe shrugs. "I guess so," she mumbles.

"So when your mom couldn't be with you, Uncle Deon took care of you, right?"

Chloe nods. She keeps thinking their time must be up, but she hasn't seen a clock anywhere. She's trying hard not to like Dr. Webster, but she's so pretty, with her long auburn hair and kind eyes and gentle smile. Plus, she's dressed nice, like the women Chloe has seen in France, with a silk scarf and beautiful leather shoes.

"What kinds of things did you do with him?"

Chloe sighs impatiently. "You know, we went to the pool or the playground, or if it was raining we'd go to the movies or something. Sometimes I just hung out at his house and watched movies if he had work to do." Chloe stretches out her legs and stares at her scuffed tennis shoes. "If he had to show a house, he'd take me with him and tell them I was his assistant."

"That's right, he's a realtor. So he probably shows a lot of houses, huh?"

Chloe rolls her eyes and nods as if this is a really dumb question. She knows she's being rude and feels a tug of guilt, but she just wants to go home.

"What was it like being with Uncle Deon?"

Chloe draws her knees up to her chest and wraps her arms around them. "What difference does it make? I just want my mom to get better!" This comes out louder and madder than she meant it to, and Chloe looks at Dr. Webster to see if she's upset.

Dr. Webster smiles sadly and says, "I know you do, Chloe." She uncrosses her legs and stands, holding out a hand to Chloe. With a brighter smile and a twinkle in her eyes she says, "Let's be done for today, okay?"

Sophie wanted to bring Chloe to this appointment, but Anthony flatly refused. To every point she argued he simply replied, "No." He expected her to be furious, but this behavior was so out of character for him that when he and Chloe left together, Sophie just looked confused.

Anthony knows that a meeting between the two women would be a disaster. If Dr. Webster were a man, there would be no problem, but she is a pretty woman (with long, beautiful hair, no less) trying to get Chloe to open up about something she won't tell her own mother. Sophie seems healthier every day, and he doesn't want jealousy, anger or frustration derailing her progress. His own impotence in this situation gnaws at him constantly, and he knows it would be far worse for Sophie.

After a few excruciating minutes in the viewing room, Anthony decides not to watch this session. Detective Hancock deposits him in the station's lounge. Anthony settles on the lumpy couch, flips open his cell phone and dials his father's number. It's eight o'clock, which means it's eleven in New York. Anthony knows his father rarely leaves the apartment before noon. Still, the machine picks up after two rings, which tells Anthony that his father isn't retrieving his messages.

Anthony doesn't hide the irritation in his voice as he says to the machine, "Dad, you're pissing me off now. Are you there? Sophie thinks you have a lady friend. I'd love to hear all about her. Okay. Please call me if you ever listen to your messages. You've got until the end of the week before I call the cops."

As Anthony closes his phone, he feels a growing heaviness in the pit of his stomach; specifically, the part dedicated to concern for his father. It is almost as leaden as the spaces reserved for Sophie and Chloe, but not quite.

Anthony reaches into his briefcase and pulls out more of his father's old letters. He grabbed a few at random this morning, and wonders where in his life he will now find himself.

Anthony,   *July 10, 1972*

You are only in the third grade, but your teacher tells us what a bright and curious boy you are. You seem to excel in every subject, and I don't think I'm biased when I say you are one of the smartest in your class. I thank the Good Lord that you got your mother's brains and not mine! Keep working hard — don't get lazy because things come easy to you.

When you're on the smaller side, the bigger boys are bound to pick on you. I promise this won't last forever, and it will be a good learning experience if you let it. You can choose not to fight without being a coward. If you get hit, stand your ground but don't hit back. If you get knocked down, get back up but don't run away. And don't be a tattletale. You may end up with some scrapes and bruises, but you'll gain the respect of your peers if you don't react the way the bullies expect.

Your sister misses you when you're in school. Now that you have your own friends, you may get tired of her following you around. That's okay, but try to put yourself in her shoes, and be as patient as you can. She looks up to you, so set a good example for her. Being a big brother is an important job, and your mother and I hope that you two will be close for the rest of your lives.

We love you and are so proud of how you've grown,
Tu Padre

This letter is a sucker punch to the stomach. Shame washes over Anthony and he feels eight years old again. The scenes play in his mind with painful clarity: being labeled the geeky smart kid, getting beaten up again and again, the hurt and betrayal on his sister's face every time he told her to leave him alone. He folds the page with shaking hands and reminds himself that he was just a child, the same age as Chloe, in fact. He had taken his father's advice and had become a better person. The values his father never stopped promoting — the desire to learn, hard work, courage, honor and compassion — have become fibers of his being, so thoroughly integrated that he had forgotten there was a time he had to be told to be nice to his sister.

He knows that the man he has become is a result of his father's gentle yet tireless guidance over the years. At work, he is often called upon to handle angry clients or contractors, because he can stand his ground without becoming contentious. He hears them out, taking their verbal blows without flinching. If they need to vent, he lets them vent. If an important decision is at stake, Anthony often simply nods in response, then waits until they are deflated by this unexpected reaction. At that point, they are no match for Anthony's sympathetic tone, unassailable expertise and utter conviction.

Anthony,   *July 10, 1974*

Ten years old! You seem less like a boy and more like a little man every day. You continue to do well in school and seem to be taking a particular interest in art. I marvel at how you love to draw and how patient and focused you are. Your mother agrees with me that your work, many of them sketches of the buildings I work on, show a talent quite advanced for your age.

I especially want to congratulate you on a job well done with your paper route. I should be so lucky to have such dedicated coworkers. Your mother worried about you taking on such a big responsibility, and even though she would never admit if she were wrong, God bless her, she is every bit as proud of you as I am.

Remember to enjoy the freedom of childhood and try not to take on too much. Roll in the grass in the park, savor a hot fudge sundae, collect shells at the beach. I wish sometimes I could slow time — your mother and I only have eight more years with you!

We love you now more than ever,
Tu Padre

    Anthony presses this letter to his chest and feels his body warmed by his father's love and, more important, his approval. He never considered it unusual for a father to show his son such unabashed affection, mostly because he had nothing in the way of comparison. Now he appreciates for the first time that his father's devotion was, and is, far from ordinary. This is the kind of father he wants to be. He slips the letter into his briefcase, and resolves to be more attentive and loving with Chloe. Maybe if he'd been paying more attention, they wouldn't be here right now.

    Just then, the door to the lounge opens and Dr. Webster appears. She smiles at Anthony and sits at the other end of the couch. "Gotta minute?" she asks.

Michael has tried Maxine on her cell phone after each of his three last patients. He wants to make sure she found her mother okay and didn't stumble into someone else's waiting town car. He figures she forgot to turn on her phone after the flight, so he calls her mother's house directly.

Barb answers the phone with a delighted, "Michael! How are you? Listen, I'm running late for a mani-pedi so let me get Max for you!" Michael listens to Barb yelling for her daughter, then clomping up the stairs and knocking on a door. After a muffled exchange, there is a brief silence.

"Hi baby," Maxine croaks weakly.

"Hungover?"

"Little bit. How are you?"

"I'm fine. I've been worrying about you all day, though." Michael sounds pissy when he meant to sound concerned.

"I must've forgotten to turn on my cell. Sorry I didn't call." Maxine stifles a yawn, then yelps, "Shit! I need to call Astrid. Can I call you back in a while?"

"Don't worry about it. I'm just glad you got there okay. Call me when you have some time."

Michael is irritated by this brief conversation, but he doesn't have time to work through it. A new therapist has rented an office on the floor and a welcome lunch is scheduled at a nearby restaurant. He's been looking forward to meeting her, as she also works with children and they will have plenty to talk about. He puts Maxine out of his mind and hurries off to meet the newcomer.

Soft Landing

When she finally gets back from the salon with shiny red nails on fingers and toes, Maxine's mother drives her out to Astrid's house. Maxine has recovered from her hangover and can't get away from her mom fast enough. She tries to tune out the incessant chatter, the inane local gossip, but something breaks through and catches her attention.

"I'm sorry, who got divorced?" Maxine asks casually.

"Jay Retter. But the divorce was almost a year ago. I was talking about that awful house he built off Bridger Canyon Road. His wife got their house, of course, and he lived in town in an apartment. That had to be awful, but I think he may have gone a bit mental, moving way out there."

At this point, they are driving on a gravel road that leads to Astrid's driveway. Astrid lives outside of Bozeman proper and somewhat off the grid. Maxine points, and her mom turns into the driveway, a curving dirt road that sends up clouds of dust as Maxine's mom hits the gas and accelerates.

"Slow down, Mom," Maxine begs, and her mom sighs and slows to a crawl as if humoring a slightly deranged person. "Thanks for driving me all the way out here," Maxine says, with emphasis on "all the way out here," knowing her mother will not see the parallel. "I'll probably stay here a night or two to help out. Will you be around Wednesday?"

The car rolls to a halt and her mom turns to her. "Of course. My baby is home." She leans and clumsily hugs Maxine over the console. Maxine, caught off guard by both the words and the gesture, remains motionless.

Maxine hops out, pulls her overnight bag from the back seat and closes the door. She hesitates and motions for her mom to roll down the passenger window, then says, "Have fun tonight, Mom." Her mom nods gaily, and then rather than turn the car around, decides to back out of the driveway at easily twice the speed with which they approached. Maxine stands and waits for the dust to settle before she turns toward Astrid's home.

When Astrid and John married, they immediately started planning their dream home. Within a year, their vision was realized and they set to work planting and populating their little sanctuary. Family money and a passion for progressive, sustainable living allowed them to fashion a lifestyle that includes solar power, organically grown produce, and a menagerie of goats, chickens, dogs and cats. What could easily have resulted in chaotic blight is instead a tranquil oasis, due to Astrid's unerring eye for things edible, useful or beautiful. Thus, strawberries serve as ground cover in places, thyme paths wind through the yard and tickle the nose when trod upon, an espaliered pear tree hugs the side of a tiny barn and flowering vines camouflage the chain link fence that keeps the goats out of mischief. The seasonal garden is lush but tidy, planted next to a small greenhouse that accommodates vegetables that need a longer growing season than this latitude provides. The goats keep their little pasture well grazed and sometimes produce milk, and the chickens provide fresh eggs and fantastic organic fertilizer. The house is built entirely from environmentally friendly or reclaimed materials and is only 1500 square feet, but is laid out in a way that flows naturally and feels both spacious and cozy.

Maxine loves it here.

The front door opens and the first to appear on the huge porch are the dogs, Ginsberg, a lab mix, and Twiggy, a rescued greyhound. They are older now, and trot slowly to greet Maxine as she hurries up the rest of the driveway. "Hey Gins, hey Twig," she calls. They circle around her and make it impossible for her to continue until she squats to give each a scratch and let them sniff and lick her. When she stands, she sees Astrid striding toward her, wearing her baby in a sling and a smile so broad that Maxine laughs and hops up and down a bit. She pushes past the dogs and skips to greet her old friend, and to meet her new goddaughter.

Maxine holds Star Charity Maxine Campbell carefully and stares at all of her tiny parts: her eyes, fringed with long, dark lashes; her upturned button nose; her plump little heart shaped mouth; her perfect ears, covered with a fine, pale fuzz. She lifts the blanket ever so gently until she can see a hand, and she studies the tiny fingers and fingernails. She wants to inspect a foot, but that would require unwrapping a complicated state of affairs Astrid called "swaddling," and Maxine knows Astrid will kill her if she wakes the baby.

Maxine inspects the nursery. The crib bedding, the baby's clothes, the curtains, the changing pad cover, a stack of cloth diapers and the blanket swaddling the baby are made of un-dyed, unbleached, organically grown cotton. The room is an ecru cloud of toxin-free tranquility. Maxine's mind flashes inexplicably to Chloe, and she wonders if she entered this world with a similarly soft landing. She hopes so.

"I'm never leaving this room," she whispers to Astrid, who is kicked back in an overstuffed rocking chair, upholstered in ivory cotton duck.

Astrid grins. She puts both hands on her breasts and winces. "My nipples are killing me. Look at this." She pulls down her nursing camisole to reveal one giant breast with an angry, red, shockingly large nipple.

Maxine gapes, then turns away and holds up a hand, but she can't resist another look. "Oh my God, they're huge!" She forgets to whisper, and she turns to watch Star nervously.

Astrid says, "You don't have to whisper. I swear a train could come through here and she'd be totally oblivious."

"Where's John?" Maxine whispers.

"He went to buy some weed. I couldn't stand the smell of it on him when I was pregnant, so he quit. He's gonna do a test run tonight. God, I've missed him like that."

John is an accountant, a complete straight arrow in every way except that he smokes dope almost every day. Only a handful of people know this, of course, or he wouldn't be trusted with too many tax returns. Maxine suspects that this is how he and Astrid can be so different and still make sense together. More than anything, Astrid loves to laugh, and when John is high, he is hilarious. He once made Maxine piss herself laughing, and she wasn't even stoned. The rest of the time, he's laid back, a little shy, but smart and kind and would do anything for Astrid. He was smitten with her in high school and he is just as smitten now. Maxine envies what they have, the ease with which they go through life together.

"Michael has been kind of a tool lately," Maxine confides. When Astrid doesn't answer, Maxine turns to see that she has fallen asleep. She knows Astrid is exhausted and is glad she missed that last remark. She's here to help, after all, not bitch about her own problems.

Maxine studies Astrid. Aside from her swollen boobs and a little paunch, she looks pretty much the same as she always has, her pretty face serene and unlined, her long arms and legs brown from hours spent in the garden, her dark hair short and spiky, as if she's just rolled out of bed. Maxine smiles to herself, picturing Astrid weeding and picking strawberries in a bikini eight months pregnant. Maxine thinks that Astrid is one of the very few people she has met who is doing exactly what she wants to in life, and is truly happy.

CHAPTER SIX

Seated before Michael is Sean, a six year old boy who witnessed his next door neighbor, a woman who occasionally babysat him, brutally beaten in her front yard by her ex husband, then shot to death before the man put the gun in his mouth and blew his brains out. The little boy's mother was in the shower and he was playing in his upstairs bedroom when he first heard the woman's screams. Throughout the entire attack, the man kept shouting, "Shut up! Shut the fuck up! Shut up, you stupid bitch!" This must have made an impression, because Sean hasn't uttered a word during the week and a half since.

His mother found out he'd seen the attack when the police arrived in response to numerous 911 calls, and one officer looked up to see Sean standing in his bedroom window. When Sean's mother got out of the shower, she heard the doorbell ringing repeatedly. She answered the door in her bathrobe with hair dripping wet, and the officer told her what had happened and that, in all likelihood, her son had seen some, if not all, of the attack. She ran upstairs and found Sean, frozen in the same spot.

She pulled him gently away from the window, lifted him onto her lap and asked him what he had seen. He stared at her. According to his mother, Sean never cried afterwards. He nods his head yes or shakes his head no, but the only time he makes a sound is when he wakes up each night screaming.

Sean is broken and it is Michael's job to fix him. He wishes his parents hadn't waited so long to bring him in, but there's no point in dwelling on that. He will use every tool in his arsenal to help bring Sean back, but he doesn't have a good feeling about this one.

"Hi Sean, I'm Michael," he begins. "I understand you've lost your voice and I'd like to help you find it. But you don't have to talk if you don't want to, okay?" Sean nods. Michael gets up and pulls from a shelf two sketchpads and a box of crayons, then walks around his desk and sits cross-legged on the floor. He motions for Sean to join him, and after a brief hesitation, Sean climbs down off the couch and sits on the floor facing Michael across the sketchpads. Michael hands one pad to Sean and takes one for himself, and then opens the box and dumps the crayons out on the floor.

"I like to draw sometimes." Michael picks a blue crayon and starts to doodle on his pad, his brow furrowed as if he can't decide what to draw. He glances at Sean and asks, "What about you? Do you like to draw?"

Sean nods. He selects a red crayon from the pile, but then just sits with the pad on the floor in front of him and the crayon clutched in his hand. Michael starts drawing a house, which seems painfully unoriginal, but he knows it doesn't matter what he draws. He glances up when he sees Sean return the red crayon to the pile and take a black one, but sees that Sean's pad is blank. After holding the black crayon for a while, Sean puts it back and picks up the red one again.

They continue like this, Michael drawing and chattering benignly, occasionally throwing out a question, like what color does Sean think the roof should be. Sean remains silent and keeps swapping one crayon for another every so often. At the end of their session, Michael has completed a ridiculously detailed house (his own) and Sean's pad remains blank.

He takes Sean back to his mother in the waiting room and says, "Good bye, Sean. Good work today." He hands his mother a card with the time of Sean's next appointment, two days from now, and asks if it's convenient for her.

She nods, and then, as if to make a point, says, "Yes, that will be fine." Then she takes Sean's hand and leads him out.

Back in his office, Michael wonders how best to proceed. He can trot out all the usual suspects — clay, sand therapy, paint, dolls, therapy animals — but he decides to ask the parents' permission to consult with Dr. Besser on Sean's case. She has a tremendous amount of experience with deeply troubled children, and is a psychiatrist as well, as he learned at the luncheon. That settled, he pulls up his next patient's file.

Maxine wakes slowly and struggles to get her bearings in the dim early morning light. She was dreaming of a crying baby. Her sister? No, wait, there is indeed a baby crying. Astrid's baby. Maxine sits up in bed in the tiny guest room. There is just enough room for a double bed, a night table with a stack of books on it, a comfortable chair and a dresser. She wonders if she should get up and see if Astrid needs help, but just then, the crying stops. Maxine smiles and sinks back into her pillow. No doubt, little Star has latched onto Astrid's giant breast and is torturing her sore nipple. Something nags at Maxine as she tries to slip back into sleep, a vague sense that a piece is missing. Just as she's progressing from coherence to random, nonsensical thoughts she realizes what it is: she doesn't envy Astrid right now.

First thing in the morning, twenty-five or thirty of Astrid's and John's closest friends and relatives gather in the back yard by a stand of fruit trees for the baby's welcoming ceremony. Since Astrid and John consider themselves spiritual rather than religious, they have chosen this as an alternative to a traditional baptism. Maxine and Eric, John's best friend from high school, are "guideparents" rather than godparents. Eric is nothing like John, in appearance or manner. He is gregarious and confident, with longish hair and a tendency to dress like a rock star, albeit a hippie rock star. Since he is in his element as the center of attention, he will perform the ceremony while Maxine stands beside him holding Star. Astrid and John stand facing them across a small table. On the table is a simply yet beautifully carved wooden box, its hinged top open. The others surround them in a circle, holding hands.

It is a perfect morning. There is a slight chill in the air and the sun glints off the dew still clinging to the trees. Maxine isn't quite sure what to expect, but she knows her role is to hold Star, and she's certain she can handle that.

Eric begins. "Today we gather to welcome a new life into our community, the daughter of John and Astrid. We are here because of our relationships to them, for we are their tribe, their circle of people. In this circle, we are bound by love and respect, and will remain so throughout the life of this precious child. We open our circle to love and support her and her parents, with the hope that they find among us all the caring and nourishment they need." He pauses and glances at Star, swaddled, content and oblivious in Maxine's arms. Maxine is beginning to feel an uncomfortable fullness in her chest, and she breathes deeply to maintain her composure. Eric continues, "On behalf of all here today, welcome to our community, Star Charity Maxine Campbell. May you grow and flourish, and bless us with your own unique energy and contributions."

The circle erupts in applause, then one by one they step forward to gaze at little Star, embrace Astrid and John, and place into the wooden box an object of significance to them, something, they hope, Star will one day treasure.

Maxine catches Astrid's eyes, filled with tears, and mouths "Beautiful." Astrid nods happily and mouths back, "Thank you."

Later that afternoon, Maxine hangs freshly laundered diapers, blankets, burp cloths and onesies on a clothesline in the sunny back yard. Astrid prefers this to the dryer, which she views as a necessary evil when the weather is uncooperative. Maxine couldn't help but note that the dryer they own is huge and top of the line, however, as is the front loading washer.

Maxine realizes that the only way she can help is to do laundry, load and unload the dishwasher, take care of the dogs and keep the house tidy. This makes sense, since Maxine is not lactating and all the baby needs is her mother's breasts every two or three hours around the clock and frequent diaper changes. John is in charge of making sure Astrid is fed and hydrated. Astrid is supposed to sleep when the baby sleeps. Right now Star is sleeping soundly in her little Moses basket in the shade of a tree, but sleep is the last thing on Astrid's mind.

"I cannot believe you didn't tell me this. How could you not have called me? I'm your best friend, Maxine!" Astrid is so agitated, she is literally hopping mad. She shadows Maxine as she moves down the clothesline, jumping from one side of her to the other. Maxine doesn't look at her; she just continues pinning little items to the line and wishing she had kept her mouth shut.

"You kind of had your plate full, Ass. Plus, I didn't think it was such a great idea to tell an expectant mom about a little girl being molested."

Suddenly, Astrid is still. Maxine senses a shift in the atmosphere, a different vibe. She turns to see tears falling from Astrid's big, brown eyes. Astrid whispers, "I'm so sorry, Maxine. It's not about me. I'm sorry you had to go through that and I'm sorry for being such a shit." She wraps her arms around Maxine and hugs her in a way that only someone who truly loves you can. Astrid's enormous boobs are in the way, but Maxine hugs her back hard, because Astrid's hugs are so cathartic and it's been way too long. They begin rocking from side to side, harder and harder, then giggling, and then they hold hands and dance like little girls between the rows of tiny, wet laundry.

"Dear God." John stares at Astrid and Maxine and shakes his head in mock dismay. He is clearly baked. Astrid holds out a hand and soon all three are dancing around in a circle with John singing in a girlish falsetto, "Ring around the rosy, pockets full of posies, Astrid, Astrid, we all fall in love."

"What does Michael think about all of this?" Astrid asks. Star is nursing, and Astrid is nibbling on edamame and juicy cantaloupe and chugging a huge glass of water. They're enjoying the balmy evening on the back porch, ensconced comfortably in deeply cushioned teak furniture.

Maxine takes a bite of a grilled vegetable sandwich John made for her and chews while she considers her reply. "I get the feeling he thinks I screwed up somehow. I mean, he's trying to be supportive and all, but it just seems so hard for him."

Astrid raises an eyebrow and opens her mouth to speak, but Maxine cuts her off. "Don't start in on Michael."

"What? I don't have a problem with Michael. He is who he is. You know I don't judge people that way. I just think he could do better." She pops a chunk of cantaloupe into her mouth and smiles.

"Gee, thanks. That makes me feel all warm and fuzzy inside."

"Come on, Max. You know I love you. You're perfect for me. And for countless men out there. But Michael needs someone who shares more of his interests. And honestly, I think he needs someone a little less... headstrong."

They burst out laughing, Astrid trying not to shake the baby too much. They had an art teacher in high school, Ms. Cunningham, a middle aged woman shaped like a pear, who adored Astrid but couldn't stand Maxine. Astrid was a gifted artist, and went on to be a fine arts major in college. Her art is all over the house, and she sells her work for ridiculous sums in the shops, coffee houses and galleries that kept sprouting up in town as wealthy Californians migrate to Bozeman. Maxine didn't care about art, however, and in high school art class she paid little attention to the assignment, preferring instead to "express what was in her heart." Ms. Cunningham didn't find this at all amusing, and never tired of informing Maxine "the world would not be a friendly place for such a headstrong girl." Astrid and Maxine couldn't help but speculate that Ms. Cunningham had perhaps read a few too many Jane Austen novels.

"Oh, I almost forgot," Astrid says with a mouthful of melon. "Guess who I ran into at the library when I went to return all of my books on pregnancy and check out everything they had on infant care?"

"I give up." Maxine knows exactly to whom she's referring, but doesn't want to play.

"Okay, I'll give you a hint. What high school English teacher did you think about every time you were fucking Kevin in the back of his station wagon?" Astrid covers Star's little ear when she says "fucking."

"I may have been thinking about Mr. Retter, but Kevin didn't seem to notice. He was too busy trying to last for more than thirty seconds."

Astrid giggles. "God, I can't believe you still call him Mr. Retter. You do know that he's only, like, six or seven years older than us, right? And divorced? And I swear he's hotter now than he was back then."

"My mom told me he built a weird house in the boonies. She thinks he's gone mental."

Astrid looks appalled. "Your mother is mental. It's a fantastic house. Anyway, I may need you to make a run to the library for me."

"Stop trying to set me up, Astrid. I'm engaged. And in case I haven't said it before, I love Michael." Maxine wishes she didn't sound so defensive.

Astrid's expression turns serious. "Tell me what you love about him. Be specific."

Maxine thinks about this for a long moment. "I love that he hired me for that project even though I was so nervous during the presentation I thought I might actually vomit. I love that he's so committed to his work. I love his generosity. I love that I can trust him not to screw around on me. And I love how he keeps me... grounded somehow, you know? I don't know who I would be without him."

Astrid nods. "Fair enough. But sweetie? You're just you, no matter who you're with. Your parents ground you when you're bad. And you're not bad. You're fabulous and you always will be. Please don't ever forget that."

Chloe and her mom are on a mission. They are looking for a birthday present for her dad, and it has to be just right. This is the first time they have been out alone together since her mom got sick, and Chloe is so excited she can hardly sit still in the car. For one thing, her mom looks like she feels fine. Also, this is something they have done every year for as long as Chloe can remember, and she couldn't stand the thought of not going this year. Now they're on their way to the mall and all she has to worry about is finding the absolutely perfect gift for her father.

Chloe's mom looks over at her squirming in her seat and smiles. "Je t'aime, ma petite fleur."

Chloe beams back and replies, "Je t'aime aussi, Mommy."

It's a huge outdoor mall, so they can't just wander around waiting for something to jump out at them. They study the sign that lists the shops, Chloe's mom throwing out ideas.

"How about a tie?" she suggests.

Chloe giggles. "Daddy doesn't wear ties."

"Good point. What about this kitchen store? Maybe a set of sushi plates or a panini press?"

"Do you think they have an ice cream maker?" Chloe asks hopefully.

Her mom scratches her head and says, "That sounds like it might be something you'd like more than your father would, no?"

Chloe blushes. "I guess so."

"There's a sporting goods store in the corner over there. What sports does your father like?"

Chloe's scrunches her face. "You mean to watch on TV or to... play?"

Her mom laughs, a girlish trill that Chloe loves. "Your dad's not really the athletic type, is he? Okay, let's think. What does your father like to do?"

Chloe thinks. "He likes to cook, but he has everything for that. He likes to read, but I don't know what books he likes." Chloe's eyes light up. "He likes to draw! And he's always running out of paper and pencils and erasers and stuff, right?"

Chloe's mom smiles, clearly impressed. "That's a wonderful idea! Let's see." She runs her finger down the directory until she finds what she's looking for. "Voilà! An art supply store. I think it's over..." She matches the number of the store to the corresponding number on the map. "There! And not too far to walk. Shall we?"

Chloe slips her hand into her mom's and walks happily by her side.

Anthony tidies the kitchen. He still hasn't heard from his father. He knows he gave him until the end of the week, but he decides if he doesn't hear from him tomorrow, on his birthday, he'll call an old friend who's a cop in his dad's neighborhood. That seems reasonable. Being checked up on might embarrass his father, but he can't be mad at Anthony for caring.

Sophie is putting Chloe to bed, and Anthony wants to make a few notes for a morning meeting. He takes his briefcase into his office, and as he pulls out a folder, he sees the letters he read at Chloe's appointment yesterday. He takes them out to put back in the box and realizes there is a third letter he didn't get to. He sits down at his desk and unfolds it. When he sees the date, he wants to fold it and stuff it back in the box, but he can't, or won't.

> Anthony, July 10, 1980
>
> *I'm afraid you've had to grow up too fast in the last couple of years, but your mother and I are so grateful for your sense of humor, your selflessness and your maturity. If we haven't told you that enough, I apologize. There is a hole in our hearts that will never go away, but you help to ease our pain every day, and I hope we do the same for you. But enough of the past. This is about your future!*
>
> *I imagine you're more interested in girls right now than anything else. Now that you're old enough to date (your mother would have you wait until you were thirty!) I think back to when I was your age and how confusing girls could be. That doesn't get much easier, I'm sorry to say, but I've learned a thing or two along the way. First, you don't have to play sports for girls to like you, at least not all girls, and the ones who go for the letterman's jacket aren't the kind of girl you want to date anyway. It helps to have common interests, so clubs or activities are a good way to meet a girl you can actually talk to. You're a good looking boy, but manners and a real interest in getting to know a girl are more important than that. I know things have changed an awful lot since I was dating, but more than anything else, I want you to learn*

now to treat girls with respect. We'll talk more later about the physical stuff, but for now, just remember to treat girls the way you would want your sister to be treated, if the Lord hadn't decided to take her so early.

I know you're itching for a car, and I wish we could afford one for you right now, but you'll have to make do with the old family beater. I'm impressed with how quickly you learned to drive, and have sure enjoyed teaching you. Maybe we'll take a spin every now and then after you get your license, just to brush up.

We love you more with each passing year,
Tu padre

Anthony doesn't absorb much after the words, "if the Lord hadn't decided to take her so early." His little sister died when she was twelve after a year-long battle with leukemia. Sophie appears in the doorway to find Anthony holding the letter in front of him, tears streaming down his face. She goes to his side and reads the letter over his shoulder, then presses his head to her heart, under her healthy breast. She kisses the top of his head.

Later, in bed, Anthony asks Sophie how Chloe seemed today. Sophie doesn't hesitate. "She seemed happy. How can she act so... normal, if something so awful has happened to her?"

Anthony thinks about how he behaved after his sister died. Children are little masters of deception when it comes to acting normal. They don't want to upset their parents, of course. And being normal means fitting in, and fitting in is what's most important to them. But he doesn't say this.

Sophie props herself on an elbow facing him and says, "Tell me again what that woman doctor said. Every word."

Anthony tries to reconstruct yesterday's briefing with Dr. Webster. "She said that Chloe is definitely struggling with something big. She's terrified of losing you, obviously, but Dr. Webster thinks there's more to it than that. For one thing, Chloe seems to believe she has some sort of control over it, as if what she does will affect whether you get better or not. But apparently that's not terribly unusual. She said Chloe doesn't want to talk about Deon, but that could be because she associates him with you being sick. And she said that Chloe is angry, but her anger seems disproportionate and misplaced. She's projecting it onto Dr. Webster, probably because she's the one asking all the questions."

"And that's what concerns her? The anger part?"

"Yes. She wants to give her a little break and then try another session."

Sophie flops back down on her back and sighs. "This Dr. Webster — do you trust her?"

Anthony thinks about this before replying, "Yes."

"Okay. Then so do I."

Michael has had a truly shitty day. On his way out of the office, half a dozen coworkers are talking about going out for drinks, and they invite him along. Normally he would decline, but Maxine is out of town and going home to an empty house seems depressing. Then Dr. Besser says playfully, "Come on, Michael. You look like you could use a drink. Not that I advocate self medicating, of course." He smiles at her and surprises himself by replying, "Why not?"

When they get to the bar Michael makes a point of sitting next to Dr. Besser so he can talk to her about Sean's case. But once they have ordered drinks (red wine for him, a martini for her) and he broaches the subject, she will have none of it.

"That does sound interesting, but if you want to talk shop, make an appointment. I'm here to unwind." The way she says "unwind" is a bit suggestive, and Michael can't help but laugh.

"You have a wonderful laugh."

"Why thank you, Dr. Besser. I assume that's your personal and not your professional opinion?"

"Call me Michelle, for Christ's sake. And yes, that's my personal opinion."

Their drinks arrive and Michael raises his and murmurs, "To unwinding."

After four glasses of wine, Michael realizes he and Michelle are the only ones from their office left at the bar. They have been flirting outrageously all evening, and he feels a pang of guilt. Then he recalls something Maxine said to the detective during their phone call: "Fiancé. We're not married yet." He thinks that could have gone unsaid.

Soft Landing

Regardless, he tells himself, he's not doing anything wrong. A little harmless flirtation never hurt anyone. So what if he's been enjoying the feeling of Michelle's knee rubbing against his thigh for the last hour or so? *I'm not married yet.*

CHAPTER SEVEN

Maxine doesn't want to leave. This is for purely selfish reasons, as both Astrid's and John's parents live in town and have stopped by to bring meals, help around the house and cuddle their granddaughter several times since she's been here. In fact, she's starting to feel a bit in the way, particularly since a friend of John's is flying in tonight from Minneapolis and they need the guest room. She knows she's being ridiculous, but she can't help but feel a little rushed. *At least I got here first.*

Maxine is packed and ready to go and now she's sitting in the nursery holding Star as if it's the last time she'll see her. Astrid stands beside Maxine, stroking her head and back sympathetically.

"Okay, little bug. It was sure nice meeting you," Maxine whispers. "You be good to your mom and dad, because believe me, you'll never know how lucky you are. I'll miss you like crazy." Star gazes up at Maxine, wide eyed, as if she understands every word, and then she squirms in Maxine's arms, makes a funny face and emits a loud fart.

Soft Landing

"That's my girl," John says from the doorway as Astrid and Maxine laugh. He's holding his keys and clearly ready to drive Maxine into town.

Maxine stands and gives the baby to Astrid, who in turn gives her to John. She hugs Maxine fiercely, crying as she says, "I love you, my beautiful sister. Please come home more often." She pulls away and wipes her eyes, then takes the baby from John and says, "Now go. I can't watch you leave, and I need to feed her anyway."

Maxine presses her forehead against Astrid's and they rock this way for a moment with the baby between them. Then she turns and hurries past John and out of the nursery, back to her own world.

It's early afternoon when Maxine gets back to her house. Her mom has a cocktail in her hand when she answers the door. After some strained small talk about the baby, Maxine senses there will be no "My baby's home!" moments tonight, and decides to make herself scarce. Since she didn't pack knowing that most newborns spit up almost constantly, the first thing she does is a load of laundry. She's kicking back with a book in her room, feeling a huge void that Astrid and her world filled just hours ago, when she hears a thunderous vibration that rattles the house. She races into the laundry room to find the washing machine shaking its way violently across the floor. She lifts the lid to stop the spin cycle and stands peering cautiously into the ringer as it slows.

"What in the name of Christ are you doing?" Maxine's mom slurs. Her foul mood fills the doorway.

Maxine sees the bloodshot eyes, the smeared makeup and the cocktail sloshing around in its glass, and steps back like a scared little kid. She recovers herself immediately.

"I'm doing laundry," she replies. "What the hell does it look like I'm doing?"

Her mom sways over to the machine and fishes around inside with her free hand before proclaiming, "There's your problem. You're unbalanced!" She moves a few articles of clothing from one side to the other and slams down the lid. The washer resumes spinning smoothly. She turns to Maxine with a look of triumph on her face.

Maxine tries to stop, but her lips twitch into a smile. A giggle bubbles forth and escapes, gaining momentum and crescendoing into hooting laughter that threatens to double her over. She has tears in her eyes, and she shakes her head apologetically as she tries to catch her breath.

"Good Lord, Maxine, what's the matter with you?" her mother demands. Her eyes narrow as if the possibility just occurred to her that she's being laughed at.

"I'm sorry," Maxine gasps, wiping her eyes. She regains control and rearranges her face into what she hopes is a serious expression, then deadpans, "You're right, Mom, that is exactly my problem. I'm unbalanced."

Her mother studies her for a moment, determined to find an offense on which to pounce. Finally, she waves her drink in the air and mutters, "I swear I don't know how you two girls get by. You can't even do laundry and your sister can't keep a boyfriend for more than a month." With that, she turns dramatically and makes her exit, spoiled somewhat by a collision with the doorframe.

Shit, Lucy. The void left by Astrid's presence and utopian existence fills with anxiety as Maxine remembers she's agreed to have lunch with her sister tomorrow.

Chloe carefully sifts flour while her mom separates eggs. This year's birthday cake will be the same as every other, angel food cake with powdered sugar icing. This is her dad's favorite and Chloe and her mom have made it together for as long as Chloe can remember. They make an enormous mess and her mom never criticizes Chloe's work or insists on doing something herself. Sometimes it ends up a little lopsided, but her father always says it's perfect, and it's delicious no matter how it looks.

Chloe's mom has been acting weird all morning. She seems to be thinking about something, and Chloe keeps catching her staring at her. She wonders if it has to do with her last visit with Dr. Webster. Her mom didn't talk to her about it, but Chloe doesn't think she did as good this time. And she's not at all happy that they want her to go back again. She wonders what she needs to do different to be done with it. How she wants to be done with it! Her mom is more herself every day. The summer is practically half over, and Chloe just wants everything to get back to normal so they can enjoy what's left of it.

For dinner, her father has requested homemade pizza pies. The first time Chloe had pizza at a friend's house, she thought there had been a mistake. For one thing, someone brought it to the door in a box. Then, the thick, gooey wedge plopped on her plate, smothered with tomato sauce, cheese and lots of meat, was nothing like she'd had at home. As far as she knew, pizza had a thin, crispy crust with olive oil, fresh mozzarella, ripe tomato slices and sweet basil. Sometimes they add roasted garlic if they had time. And when they go out for pizza, they always go to the same place, the only place her father finds acceptable.

Since then she's figured out that she doesn't eat the way most of her friends do. For school lunches, her mom might pack a ham and cheese croissant and a few fresh figs with a little bottle of sparkling water or Orangina. Her friends eat the school's hot lunch, or pull from their brown bags bologna or tuna sandwiches, cookies and juice boxes. She remembers her parents' reaction when she told them a friend's mom had taken them to McDonald's for dinner before a slumber party. Chloe didn't really like the flat, tasteless burger or the limp, greasy fries, but she'll eat fast food if she's with friends whose parents take them to those restaurants. She just doesn't tell her parents about it.

So tonight Chloe and her mom will make pizza from scratch, and maybe a salad of arugula, goat cheese and figs left over from the farmer's market. She thinks she's probably luckier than most of her friends, but she doesn't ever have them over for dinner.

Earlier, Chloe's mom helped her wrap her father's presents. Chloe knows they're perfect and can't wait to give them to him, to see his eyes light up and feel his smile warm her cheeks. She watches her mom beat the egg whites until they stay in puffy little mountains. She can't keep from hoping that tonight will help make things a little more like they used to be.

Soft Landing

Despite a thundering hangover, Michael manages to sneak into the office early to avoid seeing any of his colleagues. His headache and nausea dissipate slowly as he gulps water during his first four sessions, but nothing will extinguish his shame and embarrassment. This is so foreign to him, this anxiety about what others might think of his behavior, that he feels not at all himself this morning. He has endeavored his entire adult life to remain beyond reproach. He has, in fact, taken great pride in what a positive impression he believes he makes on people.

His relationship with Maxine has presented somewhat of a challenge. Her unpredictability and his failure to temper her headstrong nature cause him to regard her as a wild card in his personal life, but certainly not a threat to his professional reputation. Now he fears that, in such a small community, the two will prove impossible to compartmentalize. For a week now, he has worried what will happen if the unthinkable happens and she is charged with assault. Now he realizes that even subtle events might undermine his credibility at work almost as surely as a public scandal. Had he and Maxine not been at odds so often lately, had she not left town so impulsively, had she called to tell him she missed him, he's sure things wouldn't have gotten so out of hand last night. Instead, he'd been left feeling abandoned at the end of a difficult day, and he can take solace only in the fact that he simply drank too much and engaged in a little harmless flirtation.

As Michael tries to figure out how to get lunch without running into anyone in the office, an instant message silently pops up on his computer screen: "Are you in session?" It's from Dr. Besser. Michelle. *Shelly.* He sighs, knowing he can't avoid her forever, and watches his fingers type, "No." Click. Seconds later, another message: "Hungry?" Michael replies, "Famished." After a moment, there is a tap at his door and he has no choice but to call, "Come in."

She's all business. "Hey. I got a couple of sandwiches from that deli next door. Roast beef and cheddar, or turkey and Swiss?" She holds a paper bag aloft, smiling innocently.

"Turkey. Please." *So this is how we're going to play it.* Michelle reaches into the bag and leans over his desk to hand him a paper wrapped sandwich, a napkin and a bottle of sparkling water. She drags a chair from against the wall and sits in front of Michael's desk, then pulls her own lunch from the bag. She unwraps her sandwich as Michael watches, bemused.

"Okay, tell me about this mute patient of yours. This one's on the house." She takes a bite of sandwich and grins.

They eat their lunches and discuss the case, which Michelle agrees sounds like a bitch. She asks smart questions and offers Michael helpful insights, and they have almost finished eating when Michael realizes how much Michelle resembles Maxine. He almost laughs aloud at the absurdity. Then again, he's always been a sucker for leggy blonds. Where Maxine's style is casual and offbeat, Michelle's is polished and professional. For a few guilty seconds, he lets himself prefer the latter.

Soft Landing

"Cookie?" Michael looks up, thinking she is referring to him, but she's holding a small, greasy paper bag. "Chocolate chip or oatmeal raisin?"

Michael shakes his head. "No, thank you. I'm stuffed. I need to review a file before my next client." Michael gathers the remnants of his lunch and notices his hands shake slightly. *Friggin' hangover.* He tosses the paper and bottle into the wastebasket and sweeps a hand across his desk for any remaining crumbs. "Thank you, though, for lunch and for the consult."

Michelle studies him as he tidies his space, and then she collects her own things and stands. As she pushes the chair back against the wall, she says, "You're welcome. But don't expect miracles." Then she's out the door without either of them having said a word about last night.

Drained after a day of listening to his clients' problems while feeling completely unraveled himself, Michael calls Maxine and is surprised when she answers after the first ring. Equally unexpected is her obvious pleasure to hear from him.

"Thank God it's you. I need to talk to someone normal," Maxine confides. "Do you miss me?"

"Of course I miss you, baby. Any idea when you're coming home?" It's out of his mouth before he can stop it and he knows it will make her feel pressured.

"In the next couple of days, I guess. Why? Is something wrong?" Maxine sounds a little deflated.

"No, no. Nothing's wrong. It's just been a crappy couple of days, that's all. You know, busy."

"Well I'm having a swell time here. My mom's in a mood, and drunk to boot. And tomorrow I get to go spend some quality time with my sister."

"I thought you were at Astrid's." This sounds like an accusation, although that isn't his intention.

"I was, Michael, but apparently other people want to visit the baby, too, so I got kicked out. I thought I should spend at least a little time at home. Wouldn't you?"

"Of course. Was everything okay with Astrid?"

"Everything was perfect. The baby is an angel and they live in paradise. I could stay there forever. "

A pause. "That's great, Max. I'm glad you had a good time."

"Uh huh."

"Well, I just wanted to say hi. Give Lucy my love."

"Will do."

"Okay. I love you."

"You too."

Michael hangs up and sits motionless in his comfortable chair in his well-appointed office, anticipating the short drive home in his luxury car, and another night spent alone in his stylish house.

Anthony's expectations for his forty-third birthday are modest. He hopes to hear from his father by the end of the day. Later on, he wants Sophie and Chloe to believe their efforts to make him happy on his birthday have been successful and are appreciated.

Anthony spends his lunch hour tracking down his cop friend in Brooklyn, whom he hasn't seen since their tenth high school reunion. He tries the home number listed in his address book and leaves a message on the machine, relieved that the number hasn't changed. Still not satisfied, he calls the 68th precinct and leaves a message there. Within the hour, Sergeant Frank Elardi returns his call.

"Tony friggin' Scialfa. How the hell are you?" Frank yells into his cell phone, accompanied by the familiar backup singers of squealing tires, sirens and car horns. Anthony grins, a pang of nostalgia for the old neighborhood catching him by surprise.

"Not too bad, Frankie, not too bad. It's been too long, though, huh?"

"Yeah, huh? You still living on the other friggin' side of the country?"

"Still here. You haven't moved, either, I guess. I left a message on your home phone." Anthony is eager to get past this cursory update on each other's lives, but he doesn't want to be rude, especially when he's about to ask a favor.

"Yeah, still in the same place, but not for long. Anabella wants to keep trying for a girl and we're running out of room."

Anthony reaches deep into his memory of their last meeting to recall how many kids Frank has. "Two boys, right?" he asks.

"Hell no, we've got three now. Little Christopher is six, and all boy, I tell you. How 'bout you? Any kids?"

"We have a little girl, Chloe. She's eight now, and the spitting image of her mother, Thank God."

"You got that right. I remember Sophie from the reunion. You're a lucky man, my friend."

Anthony doesn't care to ponder his luck at the moment, so he gets to the point. "Listen, Frank, I need a favor. I can't seem to get a hold of my father and I was hoping you could check in on him. You remember the old apartment, right?"

"Sure. I'll swing by. Neighborhood's gotten a little rough, but your old man can take care of himself. I wouldn't worry about it."

"Thanks, man. I owe you."

"You owe me for all the times I saved your scrawny ass in high school, that's what you owe me for. But we gotta take care of family. Hey, kiss your girls for me. Especially Sophie."

Anthony grins. "I'll do that. Give my best to Anabella and your boys."

Anthony hopes he hasn't overreacted. His dad is fiercely independent and the last thing he would want is to be a burden to anyone. He may bristle at being checked up on. *He should return his goddamn calls, then.* Anthony tries to focus on one of his current project, a high-density cluster of eco-friendly town homes, but his brain remains crowded by thoughts of his sick wife, his troubled daughter and his missing father.

Late in the afternoon, Anthony gives up on work. When he appears home earlier than expected, Chloe squeals and, after a quick hug, she hops up and down with excitement while he kisses Sophie. "Daddy's home! Daddy's home!" Anthony watches Sophie smile at Chloe chanting and skipping around the kitchen.

He wishes these moments of joy could mitigate the anxiety that has become a constant drone of late, a white noise that threatens to drown out the high notes. He tries so hard to be grateful, to focus on the love and achievements in his life, but he knows that this is not his nature. He has never felt it necessary to hide his dark moods from Sophie, one of countless reasons he loves her. When Chloe was born, however, everything changed. When her innocent little face mirrors his own sorrow or tension, his heart breaks. So now, he shifts into fun dad mode, lifts Chloe by her underarms and dances her around the kitchen with a goofy grin on his face. Within minutes, he is almost as happy as he appears.

Once they've devoured the delicious pizza, salad and big slices of angel food cake, Sophie and Chloe clear the dishes while Anthony sips a beer in the living room. He thinks of his beautiful girls, both hopelessly tone deaf, singing "Happy Birthday" at the top of their lungs. On the coffee table in front of him is a collection of gifts and cards. During dinner, he felt the tension in his forehead and neck ease, and now his shoulders and upper back loosen slowly. He slips off his shoes and crosses his feet on the ottoman, and with each sip of beer, the thawing sensation progresses down his spine. Chloe hops into the living room followed by Sophie, and he wills himself to stay in this moment, to savor every bit of it and let the rest fall away for a while.

He has just opened Sophie's card, signed, "Thank God I found my one true love," and her gift to him, a beautiful book on architecture that he mentioned in passing over a month ago, when the phone rings. Anthony glances at Sophie. He picks up the phone and glances at the caller ID display, and in the moment between pressing TALK and saying, "Hello?" his brain registers that, while it's a Brooklyn area code, the rest of the number is unfamiliar. Still, he's surprised to hear a voice other than his father's.

"Tony, it's Frank. Listen, I think I fucked up. Your dad's apartment number — isn't it 3C?"

Anthony sees from the concern on Sophie's face that his expression is hiding nothing. He also notices Chloe's growing impatience at this interruption, because hers is the next gift to be opened and, as she told him during dinner, she has been waiting, like, forever.

"Yeah, that's it, 3C. Why? No answer?" He knows this is the best he can hope for.

"No, man. This is gonna sound crazy, but there's some other old fart living there. Says your dad sublet the place to him a few weeks ago — "

Anthony hands the phone to Sophie and finds the card from his father on the coffee table. The first indication that something is wrong isn't the check that slips from the card as he opens it; his father sends him money every year on his birthday. Rather, it's the amount of the check. Fifty-six thousand, three hundred twenty-seven dollars and eighty-four cents. He drops it and unfolds the letter tucked in the card.

Anthony,   *July 10, 2007*

Let me start by saying I'm sorry if you've been unable to reach me the last couple of weeks. I hate to add to your worries right now. But please try to understand and respect that this is the only thing that I could do, and know that, as you are reading this, I am at peace.

Last month I went to the doctor for some pain in my back. I have pancreatic cancer that has spread everywhere. I am dying, quickly. When he told me, it wasn't like it was with your sister. I am an old man and I have lived a full life. My good friends have all passed, your mother and sister are waiting for me, and I am ready to go. My only sadness is in leaving you and your beautiful family. But I leave you with no burdens. The apartment is taken care of, my bills are paid, I've given away or sold everything, and all the money I have is in this check to you. It's not a lot but I hope it will come in handy one day. There is no point in looking for me. I know this will be hard for you, but grieve and be done with it. Don't dwell on my death, but remember my life and get on with your own. Keep me in your heart and know that I will continue to watch over you.

I remember the day you were born as if it were yesterday, but here it is forty-three years later! You are many things — a son, a husband, a father, an artist, a professional — and a success in each role by any measure. How I've bragged about you! Come to think of it, that may be what drove some of my friends to their graves.

I know this year has been a difficult one and that you are worried about Sophie, but I will let you in on a little secret your mother told me: she has it on good authority that Sophie will be fine. Which brings me to my final *piece of advice. Your mother always used to say what a good boy you were, and I certainly wouldn't argue with her, God rest her soul. But your family doesn't need you to be a good boy — they need you to be a strong man. A good boy does what is asked of him. A strong man decides on his own what needs to be done and does it. Sophie's illness is not the last serious challenge you will face. Your girls will lean on you for the rest of your life, no matter how modern and independent they may be. Make sure they know that you can handle whatever life throws at you, and them. I don't say this to trouble you, because there is so much good in the world and you have so many wonderful years to look forward to. Just remember to treasure the good times and steer your family through the rough spots, and when you get to be my age, God willing, you will be able to look back on your life with pride.*

Hug and kiss Sophie and Chloe for me, and tell them how much I love them. And never, ever forget how much I love you. I am so proud of you, Anthony, and the man that you have become. What a lucky father I've been!

I will always be with you,
Tu padre

Anthony becomes vaguely aware that Sophie is still on the phone with Frank and that Chloe is pouting and fidgeting. He drops the letter and picks up the card, which has a picture of a wrinkled, bespectacled old man on the front proclaiming "Happy Birthday!" The inside reads,

"From one old geezer to another!" It is signed, "Love, Dad." He drops this, too, drains his beer, then pulls himself off the couch, and without a word walks out of the room. Behind him he hears Chloe's plaintive, "Daddy?" but doesn't stop, not when he's out of the house and gulping warm summer air, and not when he's halfway down the block. He just walks.

It's after midnight, but Maxine is wide awake. She wishes she'd stayed at Astrid's and slept on the couch, because being in her old bedroom gives her the creeps. Just being in this house makes her want to run away, if not physically, then at least from her own thoughts. She can't imagine why, after one dead husband and one divorce, her mother chooses to stay here. She suddenly realizes her mom had the right idea earlier — what she needs is a drink. Just a little something to help me sleep. She climbs out of bed and makes her way downstairs in the dark.

The bar in the dining room is well stocked, but Maxine chooses a bottle of Chardonnay from the refrigerator. White wine will give her a nice buzz without triggering a migraine, which is the last thing she needs tomorrow. She opens the bottle and pours herself a full glass, and takes both into the living room. She sets the bottle on the coffee table and turns on a lamp by the couch. She takes a few gulps of wine, thinking it's on the sweet side and Michael would dislike it. She doesn't mind it, though, and continues sipping as she wanders around the living room.

Her eyes settle on a framed photo on the mantel.

She walks over and peers at it in the dim light, thinking it's not that great a picture and wondering why her mom went to the trouble of framing it for display. Then it hits her. My God, this must be the only one of all of us. The picture shows Maxine's young mom and dad watching proudly as eight year old Maxine holds a baby. It's her sister, Lucy, and she gazes up at Maxine with the same rapt expression that Star had that morning. Maxine lifts the photo off the mantel and settles into the corner of the sofa so she can study it in the light.

Maxine immediately notices her mother's radiant smile. There is not a single trace of this person in the woman snoring drunkenly upstairs. Granted, twenty-five years have passed, but the pretty, happy young mother in the photo is unrecognizable to Maxine, who drains her glass and pours another.

She turns her attention to her father. She's surprised at how young he looks, and she realizes that he was in his early thirties, as she is now. Less than six months later he would be gone, killed on his way home from buying baby formula by a truck driver asleep at the wheel. Maxine almost never thinks about her father, because it's impossible to avoid wondering what her life would have been like had he lived. Astrid says wondering "what if" is the surest way to keep from enjoying the present. Astrid says a lot of kooky things, but Maxine can't argue with this one. She gazes at the young version of herself. My life isn't the one I should wonder about, anyway. My life is fine.

Maxine takes a hefty swig of wine and stares at Lucy. She doesn't really remember holding her for this photo, and the picture doesn't show much more than her little face, but Maxine summons the impressions she had holding Star for the first time. Tiny. Helpless. Fragile. Innocent. Without warning, her anger builds to the point where she can hardly breathe.

Maxine was eight when her sister was born and nine when her father died. For months after the accident, her mother was no more alive than her father. Maxine remembers taking care of Lucy those summer days her mother didn't get out of bed. Her mother's parents lived in Arizona and visited infrequently. Her father's parents were local, but his mother could only do so much when every time she looked at Lucy she saw her dead son. Money wasn't a problem for a while due to a sizeable insurance settlement. When her mom remarried less than two years later, Maxine didn't know if it was because she loved Larry, she'd run out of money or she just couldn't stand being alone anymore.

Larry was a dentist in town and seemed like a nice enough guy, and despite missing her father fiercely, Maxine thought things were looking up. A few months after the wedding when she had just turned eleven, she woke to find her stepfather sitting on her bed. He stroked her face and hair. Maxine started screaming. When her mom came running, Larry said Maxine must have had a nightmare because she had been crying in her sleep.

One afternoon a few days later, Maxine was doing homework in her bedroom when Larry came in without knocking and sat on her bed. He said her mom was grocery shopping and he wanted to talk. He patted the gingham bedspread next to him. "Take a break, Maxi." She hated that nickname, but she did as she was told. He didn't talk, though. He stroked her hair and put her little hand on his crotch, and then he tried to kiss her. She pulled away and jumped up, and when he stood she did what her father had taught her to do if a stranger ever tried to touch her or force her into a car or pull her into an alley: she kneed him in the balls with every bit of her eleven-year-old might.

The effect was immediate and exactly as her father had promised. As Larry doubled over, Maxine screamed, "You leave me alone or I'll tell my mom!"

Larry muttered through teeth clenched in pain, "Go ahead. She thinks you're nothing but a lying little shit."

Maxine ran to a friend's house. She never did tell her mom, because she had a weird feeling she really wouldn't believe her, but after that she kept a chair wedged under her bedroom door knob at night and carefully avoided Larry. The only person Maxine ever told was Astrid, after making her swear on her dead dog's grave not to tell her parents. Astrid was so mad, Maxine thought she might tell anyway, but she never did. Years later, Astrid told Maxine that not telling was one of the very few things in her life that she regretted.

When Maxine was a freshman at Northwestern, Larry and Lucy visited Chicago for a weekend as part of Lucy's eleventh-birthday present. A few moments with Lucy and Maxine knew her sister hadn't been able to fend him off. She was thin and jumpy, and her eyes had a haunted, pleading look. At the same time, her behavior with Larry was oddly intimate, almost seductive. He didn't leave them alone together for even a second, and Maxine wondered if he had brought Lucy there simply to gloat. The weekend was a nightmare. Maxine blamed herself for not showing Lucy how to kick him before she left home, for being too weak to tell their mom in the first place, for not confronting him then and there.

Then something strange happened. Once they were gone and a few days had passed, Maxine started second guessing herself. Maybe nothing was going on, after all. Maybe she was projecting her own fear and anger about what had happened to her. Lucy was probably fine. Wouldn't she have said something otherwise? Maxine went on with college life and put the entire incident out of her mind.

Every time Maxine went home for a holiday, however, her suspicions rose like bile in the back of her throat. Something was not right in that house. She could see Lucy deteriorating. Larry hardly acknowledged her mother's existence. Maxine knew she should do something. But it was too late. She never said a word to anyone. It was just so much easier not to.

As soon as Lucy graduated from high school, she moved out of the house and started working as a waitress and taking classes at Montana State. Maxine had gone to Northwestern on an academic scholarship and financial aid, but Lucy was an average student, and her mom and Larry couldn't, or wouldn't, pay for a private university. It was just a matter of months before Larry moved out and filed for divorce.

Now Maxine can't stop staring at the big, innocent eyes of the baby in the photo. They bear no resemblance to the eyes she tries to avoid every time she sees her sister. She and Lucy weren't especially close before she left for college, mostly due to the gap in their ages. Then their lives took such different directions, and they were both so busy. But the real reason they don't have a closer relationship is simple: it's Maxine's guilt. It's her dirty little secret and she carries it with her everywhere, always.

What Maxine tries not to see in Lucy's eyes is the fear, shame and, most of all, her sister's own guilt. This has always been the most difficult to live with, the fact that Lucy feels guilty about what that monster did to her when she was just a child. It compounds Maxine's guilt and keeps her from seeing the person her sister has become. She wants to, not because she should, but because she's genuinely interested in knowing Lucy. She just doesn't know how she can ever make up for being weak when Lucy so desperately needed her to be strong.

She remembers that same look in Chloe's eyes the day of the parade. It was so disturbingly familiar she didn't waste time second-guessing herself then. She wonders if she should have. Still no word from Detective Hancock on the investigation, and she knows the uncertainty of the situation is putting a strain on her relationship with Michael. The funny thing is, she's not particularly invested in being right. She just wants the little girl to be okay, and she needs some closure for herself.

Maxine pours the last of the wine into her glass and wonders how her mother could have been so oblivious all those years. Was that what it was like to be a mother? Or was that simply what it was like to be her mother? Maxine is an independent contractor for a reason. She gets in, does her job and moves on to the next project. There are no long-term commitments and no loose ends. It took Michael more than two years to convince her to marry him, and after six months of engagement they have yet to agree on a date, or even a location. Now, apparently, he has his heart set on kids. Maxine knows that this should come as no surprise, and Michael is clearly confident in his potential as a parent. Maxine, on the other hand, can't help but marvel at the naked optimism of having a child. Michael doesn't know her history, a fact that weighs on her somewhat. So there is the obvious question with which she wrestles, always alone: can she handle the responsibility of motherhood any better than her own mother did?

CHAPTER EIGHT

Anthony has never before awakened and found no reason to get out of bed. He has gotten up exhausted, grieving, stressed, angry, hungover or any combination of these, but he has always gotten up. In the balance of his life, joys have far outweighed sorrows, successes have outnumbered failures and hope has managed to overcome despair. At the very least, sheer necessity — a college exam, an important work meeting, Sophie's or Chloe's needs — has left him no choice but to get out of bed. Today, however, there is nothing. He is physically and emotionally spent. His eyelids are heavy with a paralyzing apathy.

Last night Anthony walked and walked, the warm summer air cooling rapidly as daylight faded. He walked in the darkness until he found himself at Marina Bay and couldn't go any further without swimming. He stared at Lake Washington for a long time before it hit him. *He jumped off that goddamn bridge.* Of course, that had to be it. The Brooklyn Bridge had such significance in his parents' lives that both his sister's and his mother's ashes had been thrown from it's midpoint to find their final resting place in the murky waters below. His father had simply skipped a few steps of that journey, undoubtedly to save Anthony the trouble. Sure enough, they were all together now.

Anthony walked to a restaurant and called Sophie, who had the sense to drive Chloe to a friend's house before picking him up. They drove home in silence, and once they were home and in the house, Sophie held him for a long time. Then she took him upstairs and helped him undress and get into bed. She must have picked up Chloe and put her to bed before joining Anthony, but he was sound asleep by then.

Now he can hear his girls having breakfast downstairs. Sophie is well enough to take care of Chloe without his help. His father's whereabouts are no longer a mystery to solve. He's not allowed to ask his own daughter questions about what may or may not have happened with Deon. The yuppie couple from Seattle can wait one day to see the ninth revision of the elevations for their new home. Why fight it? He burrows under the covers, deep into his anger and self-pity.

Later, he wakes to a knock on the door and Sophie comes in with a tray. She's made him a grilled ham and cheese sandwich, so it must be around lunchtime. She's included pretzels and a soda. She sets the tray on his bedside table and sits on the bed next to him.

"I called your office and told them you had a family emergency." She brushes a lock of hair out of his eyes, the only part of him visible above the covers. He nods. He can't bring himself to meet her gaze. He doesn't want to see pity in her eyes if it's there. She leans over and rests her lips on his forehead for a long moment, then gets up and slips out of the room.

Anthony closes his eyes. Before Sophie woke him, he was having bizarre, frustrating dreams. In one, he rode the escalator in a department store searching frantically for Sophie and Chloe, but he ended up again and again on the same floor: tools and appliances. He was late for work in another, but no matter how hard he pressed the accelerator, his car barely inched forward. In the last dream, the one that Sophie interrupted, Anthony was in charge of a military platoon in a vast desert. Sensing they were about to come under enemy fire, he yelled to his men, "Take cover!" when there was clearly no cover to be taken. Sophie's tapping at the door became the first shots to ring out as his men scrambled helplessly.

He knows he should sit up and eat the lunch that Sophie left, or at least get up and brush his teeth, which are furry and foul tasting, but he can't seem to move a muscle. He can't stop thinking that he'd known there was something going on with his father, but he'd let himself believe everything was okay. He remembers his dad telling him his back was bothering him, but the next time they talked, he hadn't asked him about it. He realizes that he couldn't have done anything to stop his father once he'd made up his mind, but he hates this feeling of being blindsided. And it just keeps happening. Sophie's cancer. The situation with Chloe. For a man who has spent his life trying to do good and to make a difference, this lack of control over the things that matter most is shattering. So he squeezes his eyes shut and tries hard to forget the worst part: that the man he looked up to his entire life, whose advice and encouragement over the years shaped the person he has become, was gone. And Anthony never thanked him.

"Why won't Daddy get out of bed?"

Chloe can tell that her mother's patience with her is wearing thin. Chloe has been shadowing her all day peppering her with questions like, "Why didn't Daddy just drive to the lake?" and, "Is Daddy sick from walking so much?" and, "Are we going to New York for Gampa's funeral?" and, "Will Daddy be in trouble for missing work?" and, of course, "Why won't Daddy get up?" She thinks this last one is worth repeating, because so far she hasn't gotten a good answer and she really wants to know.

"I told you, Chloe, he's sad about Gampa and just really, really tired." Last night Chloe's mom told her what was in the letter, and she understands that Gampa has died, like Gamma did a few years ago, and she won't get to see him again. Chloe is sad, too, but something else is bothering her and it finally spills out in a rush of words.

"Was it Daddy's fault that Gampa died?" Her mom stops wiping the counter and turns to look at Chloe, cocking her head to one side.

"Mais non, Chloe, of course not. Why would you ask that?" Her voice is gentle but her eyes are worried.

"I don't know. Because he's so upset. Way more than when Gamma died, right?" Chloe's mom comes over and squats in front of Chloe, taking both her hands. Chloe feels like a bug under a magnifying glass the way her mom is looking at her.

"Um, maybe not more upset, but upset in a different way. Chloe, when someone dies, it doesn't have to be anyone's fault. Unless they were killed, which is a different story. People die all the time and it's sad but usually it's nobody's fault. Old people especially. You know that, right sweetie?"

Her mom looks so serious, Chloe squirms and looks away. Her mom gently touches Chloe's chin until their eyes meet. "Chloe, it's nobody's fault that Gampa died. He was old and really, really sick. It was just his time, and he was ready to go. Okay?"

Chloe nods. "Okay. But what if you're not old and ready to go? Then the people around you help you get better, right? Or they can make you get worse."

Her mom's eyes look worried again. "Well, I think being around people who love you can help you get better. Like having you and your father around helped me get better. But I really don't think they can make you worse, no." Chloe's mom touches her cheek and pulls her into a tight hug, so tight she can hardly breathe.

When she pulls back, her mom is smiling but there are tears in her eyes. Chloe clutches at her and says, "Don't be sad, Mommy. I didn't mean to make you sad."

Chloe's mom sighs and strokes Chloe's hair. "Ma petite fleur, I'm not sad. Sometimes I just love you so much it hurts. But in a good way. And if you ever do something that makes me sad, we'll talk about it and it will be okay. Please, please Chloe, don't worry so much about me, okay? Promise you'll stop worrying about me?"

Chloe nods, but she doesn't actually say the words and she has her fingers crossed behind her back. She thinks now might be a good time to ask something she's been thinking about all day. "Mommy? Do you think if I gave Daddy his birthday present it might cheer him up?"

Her mom looks thoughtful for a moment and then replies, "You know, that just might work. But let's wait until later, okay? We'll let him get all the sleepy out of him so he can really appreciate what a great gift it is."

Chloe is disappointed, of course, but she wants to help, not make things worse. She goes to her bedroom and takes out her own sketchpad and pencils. She hopes that drawing will help her not feel so nervous. Instead, she sits and stares at a blank piece of paper, thinking about Gamma and Gampa. She loved them like crazy, loved staying in their ancient apartment in New York, loved their funny accents and the huge dinners Gamma used to cook. When they came here to visit, Chloe would sit at her bedroom window forever waiting for her dad to bring them home from the airport. They were so loud and funny and alive. And now they're both gone and Chloe can't help but wonder if, since her dad doesn't have any family left here, they might move to France to be with her mom's family.

Michael's second session with Sean doesn't get him talking, but it gets Michael thinking. At Michelle's urging, he tries sand therapy, providing a wide variety of small plastic, wood and metal figurines and a sandbox in which Sean can place pieces of his choosing. Michael makes general suggestions, such as, "Maybe your house would be a good place to start." By the end of the hour, Sean has created a rather unremarkable neighborhood complete with his parents, himself and a car in front of their house, and several other houses with various human, animal and vehicular occupants. He has not chosen a dragon or wild animal to represent any of his neighbors, just a few flashy cars and oversized houses,

The only oddity is the lot next door to his house. It is vacant. Michael wishes that this were a good sign, that the emptiness indicates that Sean no longer views the house next door as a threat. He knows, however, that where the events next door are concerned, Sean has completely shut down. When Michael mentions, with some trepidation, the conspicuous absence of a house next door, Sean stares at him, then back at the sand. In one fluid motion, he topples every figurine in the neighborhood, carefully, so that no sand spills outside of the box.

After bringing Sean to his mother and arranging their next appointment, Michael returns to his office and checks voice mail on his office line and his cell phone. He's surprised to hear Maxine's voice, clearly inebriated, apologizing for being such a bitch earlier. The message was left after two o'clock in the morning, and he wonders what she could possibly have been up to prior to her impulse to call him. It's only nine o'clock, but he decides to return the call, if only to gauge precisely how hungover she is.

"Hey. What's up? Slow day?" She sounds fine.

"Not really. I'm swamped. I just wanted to make sure everything was okay."

"Oh, right. Sorry about that message. I couldn't sleep and got a little hammered last night. When in Rome and all that. You sound bummed. Everything okay?"

Michael wants to talk about Sean but is bound by

doctor patient confidentiality. He'll have to wait to consult with Michelle. "I'm fine. You?"

"Well, you know, my mom's sleeping it off and I'm getting ready to go to my sister's. I haven't heard from Detective Hancock, so I assume they haven't had any break in the case."

Michael draws a parallel for the first time between Sean's case and Maxine's predicament. "I wish I knew who was working with the little girl."

"What do you mean?"

"Nothing. I've just been working with this little boy and it started me thinking." Michael stops himself. "Never mind, I can't talk about it."

"Oh please. You talk about this shit all the time. It got you thinking what?"

"Well, how a child can be silenced just by witnessing an act of violence. It shuts them down, regardless of what else is going on in their lives."

There is a long pause. "You think it's my fault Chloe won't talk?"

"I didn't say it was your fault. I was just thinking that if the police shrink addressed the trauma of the violence first, the girl might be able to move forward and tell them if anything was going on with her uncle."

"So even if he molested her, I'm the one who traumatized her." Maxine's voice is small.

"That's not what I meant. Please don't take this the wrong way, Max." Michael sees the light indicating his next client is here. He wishes he hadn't returned this call, or that he'd kept his thoughts to himself until he had more time to explain them properly.

"No, I think I'm getting the picture. I'm damned if I do, and damned if I don't."

This seems like a non sequitur to Michael, but he can't explore it right now. He sighs and says, "Can we talk about this later, baby? I've got a client waiting."

"Sure, Michael. We'll talk later." Maxine's usual bluster is absent, replaced with an unfamiliar air of defeat.

"Are you okay, Max?" he asks, checking the clock.

"I'm fine. You better get back to work saving all the traumatized children out there. Talk to you later." Then she's gone. Michael makes a mental note to call her at lunch and straighten out this misunderstanding.

Maxine sits in her mom's car across the street from Lucy's apartment, which is on the second floor of the bookstore she manages. Maxine finds it ironic that Lucy was such a mediocre student throughout high school, yet put herself through college and became a literary buff. It's the conversational topic on which they rely when they see each other at family gatherings, since Maxine also loves to read. Maxine knows this visit will require more than the usual level of banter, however, since Lucy is expecting her to stay for lunch.

Maxine wanders around admiring the small, funky bookstore, trying to look casual, until an older woman with long gray hair approaches and asks, "Can I help you find something?"

"Lucy? I'm actually looking for Lucy." Maxine thought she would find her working, but the woman points toward the ceiling.

"She's in her apartment." Maxine has never been to Lucy's apartment and has no idea how to get there from here. Seeing Maxine's hesitation, the woman explains, "There's an outside entrance. The stairs are around the side of the building — you can't miss them."

Maxine thanks her and leaves the store, conscious of the bell ringing over the door. She walks around the building until she sees the stairs. Making her way up, she has a sudden urge to flee, but the woman in the store will most certainly tell Lucy she was looking for her. She rings the doorbell, wondering why she agreed to have lunch alone with Lucy at her apartment rather than at their mom's house or at a restaurant. Her mom would most likely have been a pain in the ass, like a small child running amok at an adult party, but the distraction would have been a welcome buffer.

The door opens and there she is, a pretty, female version of her father. Where Maxine is fair, blue-eyed and blond, like her mom, Lucy is olive-skinned with dark hair and eyes, although they have the same build. For a moment, Maxine thinks how fun it would have been to share clothes had they ever lived together when they were the same size. That seems like something sisters would do.

"Hey, come on in. Lunch is just about ready." Lucy backs up and sweeps an arm into the apartment. Maxine steps inside and lets her eyes adjust to the light as Lucy moves past her into the kitchen. Lucy busies herself checking the contents of the oven and pulling colorful, vintage looking plates from the cabinet. "Can I get you something to drink? Water? Soda? Beer? Wine?" She stops and turns around, smiling uncertainly.

Maxine supposes she should stay sober, but then she notices Lucy's half empty glass of red wine on the counter. "Wine would be great. Little hair of the dog." She sets her purse on a chair and studies the kitchen as Lucy pours her a generous glass of pinot noir.

The room is cheerful and warm, with cabinets painted a mossy green, cream tile counters, butter yellow walls and a worn maple floor. Natural woven blinds on the windows let in light while providing privacy. Lucy's collection of pottery, grouped in various corners, and a few flowering plants under a bright window add homey touches.

Lucy grins and hands the glass to Maxine. "You and Mom get pissed together last night?"

Maxine takes a sip of surprisingly good pinot. "Pissed, yes. Together, no. When did mom start drinking in the middle of the day, anyway? Not that there's anything wrong with it." She tips her glass to Lucy, who picks up her own and clinks rims with Maxine.

Lucy tilts her head for a moment and says, "You know, I can't remember a time she didn't drink all afternoon." Lucy shrugs, and turns back to her lunch preparations, grabbing a towel and pulling something from the oven. "Give yourself the tour if you want. Should take about thirty seconds. I'll just be a few minutes."

Maxine sips her wine and wanders from the kitchen into the tiny dining room, where an old round wooden table painted a glossy terra cotta is set with placemats, napkins and flatware. The walls are a muted sage and the windows are draped floor to ceiling with raw silk the color of wheat. Dark oak floors creak underfoot.

Beyond a set of French pocket doors is the living room. Golden walls, russet drapes and a green velvet sofa strewn with colorful pillows make Maxine whisper, "Sanctuary." She kicks off her shoes and lets her feet sink into the cream shag rug underneath an antique trunk that serves as a coffee table. Candles, framed photos and stacks of books create comfortable clutter. There are several pieces of what appear to be original works of art on the walls, mostly charcoal sketches of nudes and a few colorful paintings. Maxine spies a bookcase in a corner and pads over to inspect the titles. Not surprisingly, she has read many of the same novels, but is surprised at the diversity of authors and genres her sister has included in her personal collection. Maxine is happy she's not a literary snob.

"I know what you're thinking. Why keep so many books when I live over a bookstore, right?" Lucy's voice is right behind her and startles Maxine, who turns and almost spills her wine. "There are some I just have to own, you know? Do you do that?"

Maxine thinks about the quarrels she's had with Michael over her insistence on moving boxes and boxes of books from place to place. She nods. "Michael thinks it's some sort of disorder that I should see someone about." Lucy laughs loudly, a throaty, unselfconscious sound that makes Maxine smile.

Lucy gestures to the dining room and says, "Everything's ready. Hope you're hungry." Maxine follows her from the living room, starting to slip her shoes back on and then changing her mind when she sees Lucy is barefoot. Maxine thinks that Lucy is wearing the same pair of olive drawstring chinos she had on the other day, with a black T-shirt that says "hopeful" on the front and "VirtuosiTee" on the back.

As they settle at the table, Maxine is ashamed that she even considered standing up her sister. Lucy has prepared a beautiful lunch. There is broccoli quiche, a salad of avocado, jicama and cherry tomatoes and a big bowl of quartered peaches and colorful berries. She can't imagine where Lucy learned to prepare food like this. Maxine happily leaves the cooking to Michael on the nights they don't dine out. Michael's meals tend to be on the healthy, bland side, but she can't complain since he has saved her from a life of frozen pizzas and take out.

Lucy reaches out a hand for Maxine's plate. As she dishes out a wedge of quiche and a mound of salad, Maxine sees Lucy's hands shake slightly and wonders if she's a little hungover, too. Then as Lucy hands Maxine her plate, murmuring something about saving the fruit for dessert, it occurs to Maxine that Lucy is nervous. Maxine unfolds her napkin on her lap and watches Lucy fill her own plate.

Lucy sets down her plate and picks up her napkin. She catches Maxine staring at her. "What?"

"This is really nice, Lucy. Thank you."

Lucy picks up her fork self-consciously and pokes at her quiche, protesting, "It wasn't nearly as much trouble as it probably looks like — "

Maxine interrupts her. "No, I mean it. I couldn't pull this off if my life depended on it."

Lucy meets Maxine's gaze. "You're welcome."

"Surely Mom didn't teach you to cook like this."

Lucy grins and confesses, "I dated a culinary student for a while. He was really great with his hands. Anyway, I was just so relieved not to have to go over to Mom's."

As they nibble their lunches, Maxine relates yesterday's unbalanced washer incident, much to Lucy's delight. When Maxine describes her own hysteria and her mom's confusion, they both end up laughing. Maxine catches her breath and continues, "I tried so hard to stay out of her line of fire when I saw how lit she was. And this was after she got all weird and sappy a few days ago when she dropped me off at Astrid's. She said — I swear I'm not making this up — 'My baby's home!' and *hugged* me. It was surreal, I'm telling you."

Lucy shakes her head. "She can be a mean drunk, but every now and then she's all affectionate and touchy feely." Lucy shudders. "I don't know which is worse."

"I don't even know what to expect when she's sober," Maxine confides. "Except when Michael's around. Then she behaves like June frickin' Cleaver. He really doesn't understand why I have a problem with her. He thinks she's a delight and that I've got unresolved issues."

"Gosh, you think?" Lucy jokes. They've cleaned their plates. Lucy motions to the fruit salad and asks, "Room for dessert? I have some ice cream if you want — "

"God, no. I mean yes, fruit, but no ice cream, thanks. I've been doing nothing but eating for the last three days." As Lucy scoops generous mounds of fruit onto their plates, Maxine catches a whiff of fresh mint. She bites into a juicy, sweet peach and thinks certainly she's capable of making a fruit salad.

"So how is life in the big city with Michael? Is it as terribly glamorous as I've imagined? Tell me so I can live vicariously through you." Lucy waits expectantly.

"Well, Kirkland isn't exactly a big city, but Seattle is right there. It's good. You know, the house is beautiful and Michael loves his job. I work at home so I haven't really met that many people yet." Maxine trails off.

"It's not a bad commute, though, right? I can't imagine sitting in traffic. I love closing the store and just walking upstairs. But I guess it's different when you're home alone."

Maxine nods and chews.

"And what about the wedding planning? Is that making you crazy yet?"

"Oh my God." Maxine rolls her eyes and nods, shoveling more fruit into her mouth.

Maxine is fighting a feeling that has been simmering in her gut since she walked through the door, and now Lucy is asking about her life and she can't ignore it anymore. She feels like an imposter. This is magnified by the fact that Lucy is not at all an imposter. Lucy might have gone to all this trouble, at least to some extent, to impress her, but Maxine knows it's more likely that Lucy wanted to make her feel welcome, to make her happy. Lucy's appearance, her apartment, her behavior — all are genuine expressions of who she is, and Maxine finds this lack of artifice surprising. She also finds it unsettling, because it presents the opportunity to get to know Lucy, which she always thought she wanted. She's having trouble taking advantage of Lucy's openness, however, because she isn't sure she's prepared to reciprocate.

Lucy seems to think Maxine has it all. The truth is that she has been feeling increasingly distant from Michael lately. There is no wedding planning because there is no wedding date, or location. She doesn't believe she will ever feel at home in Kirkland, where she has almost no friends. To top it all off, she may be facing assault charges any day now because a little girl reminded her of Lucy. Lucy, who believes Maxine is happy when, in reality, she's been in denial for a long while.

"Max?"

Maxine looks up. "Sorry, you got me thinking about all the stuff I need to do when I get home." She sets her fork on her plate with a clatter and lays her napkin on the table. "Can I use your bathroom?" She pushes her chair back and stands.

Startled, Lucy says, "Sure. It's through the living room, down the hall, first door on your left."

Maxine pees and washes her hands, then stares at herself in the mirror. The realization hits her suddenly: the little sister she's felt guilty about all this time may actually be happier than she is. She doesn't know whether to feel relieved that Lucy is okay, or envious that she has carved out a life that so perfectly suits her. Guilt, relief, envy. *How fucked up is this?* She almost laughs aloud. She's glad she hasn't had much wine or she'd be a mess.

When Maxine returns to the dining room, Lucy has cleared most of the dishes away and is in the kitchen piling them in the sink. Maxine takes what's left from the table to the kitchen and sets it on the counter.

Lucy peers at her. "Are you okay? My quiche didn't give you food poisoning, did it?"

Maxine grins. "No, I'm fine. I just needed to pee like crazy all of a sudden."

Lucy's eyes open wide and she brings a hand to her mouth. "Oh my God, you're not — " she stops herself, embarrassed and apparently hoping she hasn't overstepped.

It's a moment before Maxine realizes what Lucy is thinking. "Pregnant? Holy Christ, no. Bite your tongue." She lets out a hoot, and when the perfect absurdity hits her, she can't stop laughing. Lucy isn't sure what's so funny, but joins in the laughter, anyway. Once Maxine gets herself under control, she takes her mostly full glass of wine from the counter and quaffs half of it as if to make a point. "This is delicious, by the way." She drains the rest.

Lucy looks slightly anxious as Maxine sets down her glass. "Do you have to go right away?"

Maxine sees the hope in her sister's eyes and weighs it against her own urge to run away from everything she's feeling. She has never considered herself a weak person, but she's not sure she's strong enough for this. After a long, awkward silence, Maxine makes a decision that will impact her life in ways she can't imagine.

It must be dinnertime, Anthony deduces, when Sophie brings him a tray of spaghetti, crusty bread and a side of garlicky sautéed spinach. Being French, she also includes a bottle of Chianti and a wine glass. She must be truly worried about him; otherwise, the wine would be French. She sets the tray at the foot of the bed.

Anthony lies passively and watches her. After

removing his untouched lunch tray from the bedside table and setting it on the floor by the door, Sophie returns and sits on the bed next to him. "Chloe wants to give you your birthday present. She thinks it will cheer you up."

Anthony opens his mouth to speak but his dry, unused vocal chords emit a pitiful croak. Sophie pours him a splash of wine and props him up to sip it. He clears his throat and asks, "Will it?"

Sophie thinks for a moment and replies, "No. It will make you cry. I'll tell her you were asleep when I came in and she should wait until tomorrow." Sophie rises and sets the dinner tray on Anthony's lap. "Please, Anthony, eat just a little." She kisses his forehead and says, "I love you."

Once she's gone, Anthony pours himself a full glass of wine and downs it with a piece of bread. He picks up a fork, pushing the spaghetti puttanesca around his plate. *Whore's pasta.* He spears a few olives and capers, figuring he might as well eat his vegetables. Or are they fruit? He ponders this as he pours a second glass of wine and soaks up some olive oil and anchovies with another piece of bread. He tries to twirl some noodles around his fork, but he's too lazy to pick up his spoon and his stiff hands can't win this battle. *Battle.*

Anthony's dreams are monopolized by war. They involve everything from hand to hand combat to nuclear explosions. At first, he woke up frightened. As the dreams continued, his feelings upon awakening progressed from fear, to anger, to vengeance, and finally, to outright bloodlust. He takes an enormous bite of spinach and has a fleeting image of Popeye's bulging biceps. Another swig of wine and he imagines Chloe, his little ray of sunshine, in her bedroom fretting because she must wait until tomorrow to give Daddy his present. Is he such a coward that he can't face his own daughter to give her some peace of mind? *Your family needs you to be a strong man.*

When Anthony reaches the bottom of the bottle, he knows what he has to do. He can't believe it has taken him this long to see it. For a week now, uncertainty has masqueraded as the adversary, while the real enemy lives less than a mile away.

Anthony climbs out of bed and dresses quickly, knowing he has a window of opportunity while Sophie gives Chloe her bath and puts her to bed. He opens the bedroom door and listens, making sure they are both upstairs, then he carries his shoes to the kitchen before putting them on. A sudden wave of doubt prompts Anthony to reach above the refrigerator for a bottle of Scotch. A few swigs rekindle his resolve, and he replaces the bottle and slips out the garage door. His first inclination is to drive, but he quickly realizes what a disaster that could be. He pockets his keys and exits through the side door.

Less than fifteen minutes later Anthony stands in front of Deon's house. It's an unassuming ranch, but Anthony knows it's quite the bachelor pad inside. He remembers feeling jealous of Sophie's history with Deon when they first moved here, but when he talked to her about it, she laughed and said Deon might have had a crush on her in high school, but that was ancient history. Since then, he and Deon have become friends. Sometimes Anthony wonders why a man pushing forty hasn't married and started a family, but Deon prefers to play the field and assures Anthony that he does okay. Anthony has, from time to time, envied Deon his freedom, but standing unsteadily in front of his house under the current circumstances, he is disgusted by Deon's frat boy mentality. It all makes sense now, and in Anthony's inebriated condition, he speculates that Deon has simply transferred to Chloe his unrequited love for Sophie.

This repugnant notion is enough to propel him forward, and in a minute, he stands in the doorway face to face with Deon, who is understandably confused and, Anthony believes, nervous. Deon stands a good head taller than Anthony, but this in no way dampens his determination.

"Tony? What the hell...?"

Anthony pushes past Deon into the house and stands in the foyer, swaying slightly, distracted by the chaos confronting him. Pizza boxes and other take out containers, dirty dishes, beer bottles, soda cans, newspapers, and a shitstorm of clothes litter the living room. There's an odor he can't quite place, but it reminds him of college.

"What are you doing here, Tony?" Anthony turns to Deon, who attempts to mask his discomfort behind impatience and irritation. Deon is generally good-natured, which makes his size less daunting. Now, however, Anthony realizes no matter how drunk and angry he is, he's no match for Deon physically. He wonders how the hell that woman managed to knock him out. *Your family needs you to be a strong man.*

"Did you do it, Deon? Just between us. I need to know. Sophie needs to know." His voice, which he imagined confident and intimidating on the walk over here, comes out unsteady and whiny instead. He sees it in Deon's expression; he betrayed his weakness the moment he opened his mouth.

"You shouldn't be here, Tony. Jesus, you're drunk." Deon doesn't even appear angry, just pained and eager to be rid of him. Anthony feels as effectual as a mosquito buzzing around someone trying to sleep, a nuisance at which to swat, or even worse, to ignore by covering one's ears with a pillow.

Anthony tries to embody the strong man his father brought to life over the years. He struggles to stand firm, to prevail with his intelligence, courage and steadfast refusal to resort to violence. Instead, he succumbs to the years of schoolyard bullies, the intractable clients, the steady drone of anxiety. With a roar, he rushes Deon with every ounce of his pent up fury and pins him against the wall of the foyer. His hands encircle Deon's throat, albeit above his own line of sight, and his thumbs dig into his trachea. Deon's eyes bulge with genuine fear. Were he not struggling to regain his footing, lost when his ass slid atop a narrow metal and glass hall table, Deon surely would have flung Anthony across the room. Instead, he flails helplessly, gasping for air. While it lasts, Anthony relishes this feeling of power, of intimidating rather than being intimidated.

"You think you can fuck with my family and get away with it, you goddamn piece of shit?" Anthony spits. "If you touched her, if you even thought about touching her, you better hope the police get to you before I do."

At this point Anthony can no longer hold Deon aloft, and as he watches him slide down the wall, he knows he will pay for the humiliation he caused. He backs away and turns toward the front door, but just as he grasps the knob, he feels Deon's hand on the back of his head. With one forceful push, Anthony's face meets the wooden door and he tastes warm blood in his mouth. He tries to open the door, but Deon grabs his wrist and wrenches it away. Anthony is sure Deon will beat him to a pulp right here in the foyer, and wonders what he'll do with him after that, but instead the door is flung open and Anthony feels himself become airborne. He lands in a heap several yards away on the front walk, and covers his head with his arms to ward off the blows that are sure to follow. Rather than Deon's fists, feet or even words striking him, however, there is nothing but the sound of the front door slamming and his own ragged breathing.

Maxine is curled at one end of the welcoming sofa, her feet tucked under her. Lucy forages through an extensive music collection, looking for a CD she wants Maxine to hear.

"Astrid says you can tell a lot about a person by how they listen to music," Maxine offers. Lucy glances up, one eyebrow arched. "She says if you look for the next CD while one is playing, you're focusing too much on the future and missing out on the present, which is, of course, the ultimate sin as far as she is concerned. If you pick a bunch ahead of time and load the CD changer, you may be so preoccupied with planning ahead that you aren't flexible enough to go with the flow."

Lucy smiles fondly. "Let me guess: Astrid listens to CDs one at a time and then chooses the next one depending on what color her aura is?" Lucy finds what she's looking for and holds it aloft victoriously.

Maxine knows Lucy likes Astrid and isn't making fun. She smiles and says, "Something like that."

Lucy pops the CD into the player and adjusts the volume. She crosses to the couch and sinks into the cushions, stretching out her long legs and crossing her feet on the coffee table. Maxine is aware that they are feigning a level of familiarity and comfort that is entirely wishful thinking. Still, it feels like progress, whereas bolting out the door after lunch would not have felt right at all.

"Oh yeah, I remember her," Maxine says after listening to the music for a moment. "Didn't she play at dances and coffee houses and churches?" Lucy nods, grinning.

They sit silently, Maxine casting about for some nugget with which to start a conversation. "Have you seen that picture Mom has on the mantle? I stared at it for an hour last night and drank a whole bottle of wine."

Lucy turns to Maxine, her brow furrowed. "Which one? She has some sort of rotation system going. But she looks great in all of them, naturally."

"The one of her and Dad, and me holding you when you were a baby. I think it might be the only one of all of us." Maxine wonders if this is insensitive, potentially upsetting to Lucy. But Lucy doesn't look upset. She just thinks for a moment and then nods.

"Oh yeah. She's had that one up for a while now. She got all pissy when I asked who it was. I mean, I would've figured it out eventually. I've seen other pictures of you all. I just hadn't looked at it that closely."

"It's weird, isn't it? How different Mom looked then?" Maxine hasn't been able to get her mom's blissful expression out of her mind. It keeps flashing in her head, like a warning not to get too comfortable, because before you know it your perfect life could be flattened under an eighteen-wheeler.

"Yeah, I guess. I wonder more about Dad, though." Lucy hesitates, and then asks, "What was he like? I mean, I know you were little, but what do you remember most about him? I don't remember anything, obviously."

Before last night, Maxine hadn't thought about her father for so long, she wonders if her memories of him are reliable, or even accessible. She's not sure she likes the direction this conversation is taking, but she figures she started it and owes it to Lucy to make an effort.

"Well, he worked hard so he wasn't around much. You know he owned a hardware store, right?" Lucy nods. "But when he was around, he was fun — not one of those grumpy dads that just wanted to be left alone with his newspaper. He wasn't afraid to act silly when he played with me, and he didn't talk down to me, you know? He'd show me stuff, guy stuff, like how to hammer a nail, or he'd take me to the hardware store with him sometimes and explain what all the different tools were for. I think he knew mom would teach me the girl stuff, and he wanted to teach me some of what he knew, too."

Lucy nods somberly, taking it all in. "What were he and Mom like together?"

Maxine really has to dig for this one. "I think they were just happy. They had a family and friends and probably didn't have to worry about money." Maxine smiles as a vivid memory floats to the surface. "Every day when he got home from work, he'd wrap Mom in this big bear hug and lift her off the floor. She always giggled. Then he'd pick me up do a little dance, and he always smelled nice." Maxine's voice catches and she clears her throat.

"I'm sorry. You don't have to — "

"No," Maxine interrupts, laughing it off, "it's fine. I just hadn't thought of that in so long."

"I can't ask Mom anything, she's such a nut job, but I'm just so curious sometimes. I'm lucky you were so much older than I was, I guess."

Maxine feels the beginnings of a headache, a dull ache above her left eye and at the base of her skull. It's time. Before she has a chance to change her mind, her mouth is open and the words are flying out. "How can you think you were lucky? My God, Lucy, I left you in that house and never looked back. I didn't warn you, I didn't help you, I didn't even keep in touch. I just let it happen. I'm sorry, Lucy. I was old enough to protect you and I should have. I don't why I didn't do something, I really don't. I'm so sorry."

Lucy pulls her knees to her chest and hugs her legs, then stares straight ahead, expressionless. "We don't have to do this, you know. I'm sure you've learned in therapy that what happened to you wasn't your fault. Why should what happened to me be your fault? Anyway, I'm fine. I mean, I'm fucked up, mostly where guys are concerned, but I'm working on it."

Maxine has a sick feeling and wants to get up, leave Lucy's apartment and drive away, now. But she has to hear it. "What do you mean, what happened to me?"

Lucy stares at Maxine, obviously confused. When she replies, her tone is that of someone dealing with a particularly slow child. "What that sick bastard did to you. You have been in therapy, haven't you?"

Maxine can't believe that she didn't see this coming, that the possibility hadn't occurred to her years ago. "Oh my God." Maxine pulls her feet out from under her and leans forward, her elbows on her knees and her head in her hands. "Holy shit."

"*What?*" Lucy's confusion gives way to impatience.

Maxine wonders if it might be kinder to let Lucy go on believing her version of the past. To disabuse her of this misconception seems cruel, particularly now, when they are on the verge of forging a friendship. Maxine doesn't want to derail their progress, but she doesn't know how to be truthful without hurting Lucy, possibly to the extent where friendship is no longer possible. Yet, she knows she can't add this enormous lie to her list of failures where her sister is concerned, even if it is a lie of omission and her intentions are good. She stayed here today to clear the air, to let honesty and, she hoped, forgiveness, make room for a fresh start between them.

"Maxine, please. What?" Lucy's voice is small and unsure.

Maxine turns to Lucy but looks away quickly, because the eyes she sees are the same eyes that have haunted her for so long. She stares at her hands in her lap, and forces herself to just say the words. They come out in a dull monotone.

"It didn't happen to me, not really. The first time he tried was in the middle of the night and I screamed and

Mom came running in. The second time Mom wasn't home and I kicked him in the balls and ran to the neighbors'. That's something else Dad taught me that I should have shared with you. Anyway, after that I kept a chair under the knob of my bedroom door and stayed as far away from him as I could. Mom didn't have a clue." Maxine sucks in air and expels it in one long, shaky breath. Lucy doesn't say anything, and when Maxine glances at her, she's still curled tightly into a ball but her head is turned away slightly, obscuring her face. Maxine continues, "I had no idea that's what you believed — "

Lucy turns to her with a withering glare that immediately silences Maxine. "Well. Fuck me." Lucy's arms and legs unfold suddenly and she gets up and strides to the other corner of the room, as far from Maxine as possible. "I didn't just believe it because I'm an idiot, you know. I believed it because that's what he told me," she spits.

Maxine gets up and starts to walk slowly toward Lucy. The tightness at the back of her throat makes it difficult to speak, and when she does, her voice is as wobbly as her legs feel. "I'm sorry, Lucy. You said it, he was a sick bastard and it wasn't your fault — "

"Just stop. I don't need you to tell me that. And stop saying you're sorry. Stop being sorry for me. I mean, that's it, isn't it? Poor Lucy, too stupid and weak to defend herself like clever little Maxine did."

"No." Maxine can feel the tears welling no matter how hard she tries to stop them. She takes a few more steps toward Lucy, who is beginning to look like a cornered animal. "That's not what I think. I've never thought that."

She clamps her mouth shut, but the sob escapes from her nose instead. And just like that the dam breaks, and there's nothing she can do to stop the flood.

"Are you crying?" Lucy asks incredulously. "What do you have to cry about, with your perfect fiancé and your perfect house and your perfect fucking life? I hope you're not crying for me, because I'm fine. Probably not according to your high standards — "

"Lucy, don't, please." Maxine closes the remaining space between them, sobbing openly, and reaches for Lucy. Lucy backs into the wall and holds her hands in front of her to keep Maxine away. Maxine grabs Lucy by the shoulders and pulls her towards her, but Lucy flails at Maxine's chest. Maxine is caught off guard, and her surprise gives Lucy the opportunity to slap her face, hard. Both are momentarily stunned, but Maxine recovers and wraps her arms around Lucy, holding her tight until she stops struggling. Lucy remains stiff for a second, then drops her head on Maxine's shoulder and drapes her arms loosely around her waist. Maxine feels Lucy's body start to shake and realizes she's crying, too. They remain like this, clinging to each other and crying, until Lucy gasps, "Oh my God, I hit you. I'm so sorry." This brings a fresh burst of wailing from Lucy, but Maxine's weeping subsides. She takes a deep breath, her tears and her emotions drained. She strokes Lucy's hair and waits for her to quiet. Then, without warning, a giggle bubbles in Maxine's throat. Lucy pulls away and wipes her eyes and nose. She peers at Maxine warily.

"You hit me." Maxine chuckles again as she wipes her own face, touching the reddened spot on her cheek.

Lucy's mouth twitches into a grin, and then she laughs. "I don't think I've ever hit anyone before. I'm totally sorry. Does it hurt?"

"Not really. I could kick your ass, by the way. I'm trained in self-defense. And facing possible assault charges back at home."

Lucy gawks. "Are you kidding?"

Maxine runs a hand through her hair. "Long story."

Lucy studies Maxine curiously, then says quietly, "Tell me."

Lucy doesn't say much during the recounting of the Chloe incident, but her eyes fill with tears when Maxine confesses her uncertainty. Lucy shakes her head violently and says, "Don't do that to yourself. Even if you were wrong, which I'm sure you're not, you did the right thing." Then she takes a deep drag on a joint and passes it back to Maxine.

"Max?" Lucy's voice is hesitant. Maxine looks up as she inhales deeply. "This little girl, Chloe, won't tell anyone what happened. I didn't tell anybody what was happening. Why didn't you tell Mom what he did to you?" The question hangs in the air with the pot smoke and smell of scented candles.

"I didn't think she would believe me. He said she thought I was a lying little shit."

Lucy nods. "Me too. That, and that you never told."

Maxine is enjoying a surprisingly mellow high along with a pint of ice cream. The past and all of the drama at home seem distant and not at all worrisome, but she's ready to change the subject. She exhales a cloud of smoke, sinks deeper into the couch and gazes at the boldly erotic sketches and colorful abstract paintings on the walls. "I love your art. Michael has some sort of boner for black and white photography, but I'd like more variety. Did you buy them here?"

"They're mine. Well, the nudes anyway. I took one of those classes where they make you draw every friggin' part of the human body from every angle. With models and everything. You'd think it'd make you horny, right? But it just made me fascinated by all of our weird parts. And I realized that saggy boobs and crooked pricks are beautiful in their own unique way."

"Crooked pricks. That'd be a great name for a band." They giggle. "Seriously, though," Maxine continues, "they're really good." She takes another hit and returns the joint to Lucy, who sits at the other end of the couch.

"You can take one if you'd like. I've got plenty more. You can look through them and pick your favorite. Or whatever you think Michael would like. Some guys are a little weird about nudes. They don't really want to see pubic hair hanging on their wall."

Maxine tries to hold in her last drag, but she laughs and coughs so hard her eyes fill with tears.

Lucy grins and says, "I don't mean actual pubic hair, you understand." She snuffs out the joint and lays it on the coffee table, then takes the ice cream from Maxine and leans back. "So Michael is a bit of an art dilettante?"

Maxine replies, "Uh, I guess so." She hesitates before asking, "What does that mean, dilettante?"

Lucy thinks about it and says, "Huh. I don't really know." She jumps up and runs to the bookshelves.

Holding the ice cream in one hand, she pulls a gigantic dictionary down with the other. On the way back to the couch she mutters, "Sounds too much like debutante." She sets down the ice cream and sits on the couch with the dictionary in her lap, flipping pages until she finds it.

"Here we go, dilettante." Lucy glances up to make sure Maxine is paying attention. "Dilettante: 1) a person who takes up an art, activity, or subject merely for amusement, especially in a desultory or superficial way; dabbler. Or, 2) a lover of an art or science; connoisseur; member of the intelligentsia or cognoscenti." Lucy peers at Maxine, her brow furrowed. "Oh, of course. It means either an amateur or an expert." Lucy sets the dictionary on the floor and retrieves her ice cream from the table.

Maxine, still giggling, wipes her eyes and says, "God, I'm a mess and getting fatter by the minute. I want you to know that I hold you personally responsible." Maxine points a finger at Lucy, and at precisely that moment Lucy lets loose a loud, protracted fart.

Lucy takes a bite of ice cream and with her mouth full says, "You shouldn't point. It's rude."

Maxine laughs until her sides hurt, then her smile fades and she says quietly, "You know, I think with all the great sex and the fun of the chase and the engagement and all, I may have overlooked something about Michael." Maxine feels as if someone else is talking through her, as if these words are a test run and won't count later on.

Lucy tilts her head and asks, "What's that?"

Maxine pauses, searching for just the right words. "I think he might be kind of an asshole."

CHAPTER NINE

Maxine wakes on Lucy's sofa and for one brief moment is blissfully unaware of where she is or what is going on in her life. She simply feels good, stretching luxuriously with the abandon of a cat waking from a particularly restful nap. Then she opens her eyes and looks around Lucy's living room and the events of yesterday and last night come flooding back. Instantly, she is overwhelmed by the awful drama of it all. Her mental recap confirms that each moment was indeed more embarrassing than the last: crying hysterically, forcing Lucy to hug her, revealing her doubts about Michael. That was the worst of it. She thought she was just high and thinking out loud, but once she got going, she shared doubts and fears she had never even explored in her own mind. She cringes and turns her body toward the back of the couch, closing her eyes and pressing into the crevice as if attempting to disappear.

"Cut it out." Maxine jumps at Lucy's voice and turns to see her striding into the living room with two cups of coffee.

"What?" she mumbles, sitting reluctantly and accepting a steaming mug. She pulls her knees to her chest, making herself as small as possible, hoping to disappear into the cushions.

"Stop feeling all weird about yesterday. We promised we weren't going to do that." Lucy sits on the floor in front of the coffee table across from Maxine.

"I'm not," Maxine protests lamely.

"We promised we were going to be honest with each other from now on, too," Lucy challenges. "Anyway, if anyone should feel weird, it's me. I was totally spastic." She waves her arms around in front of her as if fighting off an attacker. Maxine giggles. Lucy continues, "At least you didn't wake up in bed remembering all the crazy sex you had last night but not the name of the guy next to you."

Maxine considers this. "You're a little bit of a tramp, aren't you?" she teases.

"Little bit," Lucy replies, grinning. "If it weren't for the college, I'd have to move."

"Gross. I was kind of a slut before I met Michael, but at least they could buy me a drink." Maxine realizes that she has no reason not to trust her sister, who seems like a genuinely cool person. "Okay, no weirdness. We're sisters. We might as well start acting like it."

Lucy smiles. "I'd like you if you weren't my sister. I think we'd be friends."

For a horrifying moment, Maxine thinks she might cry again, but it passes. She smiles back at Lucy. "I think so, too."

Lucy fixes a yummy breakfast of cheesy omelets and leftover fruit salad, then showers, dresses and heads down to open the bookstore. She tells Maxine she is welcome to have a shower and help herself to a change of clothes. Now Maxine stands before Lucy's closet in her underwear, a bath towel wrapped around her wet hair. She's reminded of her dream on the flight, except she has no feelings of malevolence or fear, and Lucy's clothes are a lot like her own and fit her perfectly. She finally decides on a deep v-neck black T-shirt and low slung khakis. *This really is fun.*

Once she's dried her hair and played with Lucy's makeup, Maxine makes her way down to the bookstore. Walking through the front door, she can't help but feel as if she's gone though some sort of metamorphosis since yesterday. The gray haired woman is behind the register, and when she sees Maxine, she smiles and points. "She's in historical fiction."

Maxine is almost surprised the woman recognizes her, but she returns the smile and says, "Thanks." She makes her way through the rows of books, and is distracted by the literature section before she finds Lucy. She pulls a new novel by one of her favorite authors off a shelf and is reading the reviews on the back when a voice behind her makes her heart slam.

"It's his best one yet, I think."

Maxine turns and smiles up at Jay Retter, her high school English teacher. Astrid was right; he's still absurdly handsome. Aside from a slightly receding hairline and deeper crinkles around his eyes when he smiles back at her, he hasn't changed much. When Maxine speaks, she's relieved her voice doesn't betray how nervous she feels, but she hugs the book to her chest to keep her hands from shaking. "I can't buy it, though. I've imposed a moratorium until I've finished all those books I just had to have before they came out in paperback. It could take years."

Jay's smile widens. "It's good to see you, Max." He lays a hand on her shoulder, a gesture that used to excite her so much she thought she might throw up. Now she just enjoys its warmth and is glad she showered and changed.

"You too. Astrid had her baby, you know. A little girl. I'm her godmother." The intentional inaccuracy strikes her as disrespectful, and she regrets it. She asks, "What does that mean, exactly? I forgot to ask before I agreed."

Jay removes his hand and scratches his chin. Maxine's shoulder tingles. "I believe it means you're responsible for guiding her on her spiritual path through life."

"Oh, no. Really? But I'm not at all qualified." Maxine feigns horror.

"I wouldn't worry too much about it. It's really just an honorary position. My kids' godparents don't spend a whole lot of time on the God part. Or on the parenting part. I'm not sure what they do, after the baptism." Maxine feels awkward at the mention of his children, and can't think of anything to say in response. She doesn't want to talk about Star's welcoming ceremony. It was beautiful and moving, and Maxine doesn't want to make a joke of it, which is her natural inclination.

Jay reaches out for the book Maxine is holding, and she's relieved to see that she's not visibly shaking when she hands it to him. He studies the book's cover and runs his hand over it. "You really shouldn't miss this one."

"So is this what you do with your time during the summers? Hang out in bookstores telling people what to read?" Maxine crosses her arms in front of her but is then intensely aware of the cleavage this creates, visible in the deep v-neck of her T-shirt. She uncrosses them and rests her hands on a shelf behind her, leaning back awkwardly.

"Sorry. Annoying habit." He looks genuinely embarrassed and Maxine wishes she could take back her words.

"No, not at all. I was just kidding. Of course I want your opinion." Maxine has a tendency to be bitchy when she's nervous, and then overcompensate by being obsequious. Before she has a chance to do any more damage to this conversation, Lucy appears.

"There you are. Hey Luce, you remember Mr. Retter, don't you?" Maxine asks brightly.

Lucy looks at her strangely, then nods to Jay and says, "Hey, Jay." They grin at each other and Jay turns to Maxine.

"Please tell me you didn't just call me Mr. Retter?" he asks. Lucy giggles.

Maxine rolls her eyes and tries to hide her embarrassment with a little white lie. "Sorry, I'm an idiot. I couldn't for the life of me remember your first name." This is ridiculous, considering how many times she's seen him since high school.

Jay nods slowly. "Don't worry about it. It happens all the time. It just makes me feel old."

Lucy laughs. "Dude, you are old."

Jay makes an exaggerated show of looking wounded. Maxine wants to disappear, but changes the subject to the first thing that comes to mind.

"So everyone's talking about this house you built. Astrid says it's fantastic." Maxine hopes he doesn't ask who else has been talking about it.

"It's nothing fancy, but I love it. It feels like home, you know?" He's looking at Maxine when he says this, so she nods.

"Oh yeah, absolutely. That's what it's all about, right?" *Christ, I sound like an idiot.*

Lucy protests, "Nothing fancy, my ass. It may not be big, but it's über cool. All hip and green and stylin'." Maxine is beginning to wonder about Lucy's relationship with Mr. Retter, when Lucy turns to Maxine and explains, "I dropped off some books a few weeks ago when he wasn't there and peeked in the windows." She turns to Jay. "Sorry, but it's all friggin' windows." To Maxine she says, "You really should go see it. It's totally worth the trip out there."

"How long are you in town?" Jay asks casually. Suddenly Lucy spots a customer, apparently visible only to her, and excuses herself quickly, muttering, "Talk amongst yourselves. I'll be back in a smidge."

Maxine isn't sure why Mr. Retter is asking this, so she tries to sound equally offhand. "Couple more days. I've been here since Monday."

Jay nods. "If you want to see the house, you're more than welcome. He pauses, smiling. "I think you'd really like it." This doesn't sound like a come on, just a friendly invitation.

"I'd love to see it," Maxine says evenly. "It would have to be tonight or tomorrow, though. I have to bring my mom's car back and give her a chance to use it before I, you know, ask to borrow it again. If you have big weekend plans — "

"I don't. Come tonight. I'll grill something."

"Okay."

"Okay." Jay starts moving away slowly, walking sideways, with his back against a wall of books. "I guess I'll see you later, then."

Maxine finds Lucy guiding a nervous teenage boy to the Gay and Lesbian section. Once she deposits him in the appropriate aisle, Lucy leads Maxine to a deserted reading corner. They sit on a comfortable, vintage sofa. Lucy raises an eyebrow.

"What was that all about?"

"Nothing. But I'm going to see his house tonight, thanks to you. Really subtle, by the way."

Lucy grins. "Well, have fun. I'll need details. When are you going home, anyway? Will I see you again or should we have a big dramatic goodbye?"

Maxine rolls her eyes. "I'll call you."

On her way out Maxine passes the checkout, and the older woman waves a hand to get her attention. She picks up a book and hands it to her.

"Jay said to enjoy it whenever you can. Would you like a bag?"

Maxine shakes her head, her cheeks reddening. "No thanks."

Maxine desperately wants her mom to stop yelling. She's tired from her late night with Lucy, and would like to take a nap and get her thoughts in order before tonight, as she has no idea what to expect. But Barb is on a roll, and Maxine can't seem to stop arguing with her. It's just so easy, and she has some pent up anger after her exhaustive dissection of hers and Lucy's childhoods.

"Really, Maxine, did it occur to you that I might need the car? That I might have plans?"

"Did you have plans?" Maxine asks innocently.

"No, but I could have," her mom sputters.

"You could have called my cell phone," Maxine suggests benignly.

"I did call your cell phone. Several times. I got your voicemail and I left messages. I even called Lucy and there was no answer, so I left a voicemail with her, which she didn't return. You know, I really don't appreciate you treating me as though I'm some sort of imbecile."

Maxine winces as she recalls turning off her cell as she entered the bookstore, at the request of a very polite sign. And Lucy ignored her phone all night. Score one for Mom.

"What the hell do you have a cell phone for if you don't use it? You do know how to use it, don't you? You could have checked your messages. You could have called me. Really, Max, what were you thinking? I was worried sick." *Bingo.*

"You were worried? Really, Mom? What exactly were you worried about?" Maxine's half-hearted defense instantly becomes a ruthless offense, her voice quiet and steely. She stands tall and faces her mother.

"What? What do you mean?" Her mom is genuinely confused.

"Were you worried I was kidnapped, or too drunk to find my way home? Did you think Lucy and I were out behaving badly? Or were you maybe more worried that we were reminiscing about growing up? You know, talking about the good old days."

"What the hell kind of question is that? Why would I care what you two talk about?" Her mother waves her hand in the air dismissively.

Maxine takes a few steps toward her mother. "It must've been kind of a strange feeling for you, all that worrying. You sure as shit didn't worry about us when we were little and it might have done some good."

Barb's eyes narrow and she starts to nod her head slowly, a knowing smile — more of a grimace, really — twisting her mouth. "That's it, isn't it? You ungrateful brats were whining about what an awful mother I was. You know, Larry warned me about both of you. Don't think for a second I didn't hear all the lies you told him about me. Everything I went through after your father died, and all you could do was complain to that stupid prick — " Her voice catches and she sinks suddenly into the same corner of the sofa Maxine occupied two nights ago. She stares at the photo Maxine left standing on the end table.

Maxine can tell by her expression that her mother doesn't recognize herself any more than she or Lucy did, that all she sees are ghosts. She tries to imagine what was going through her mother's mind when she framed that photo. She probably envisioned telling visitors, "Oh that. That's me and my late husband, Richard, and my two girls. Maxine was about eight or nine, I think, and Lucy came along much later, of course..."

That's when Maxine realizes that they were all victims, victims of her father's death and of Larry's abuse and lies. Her mother may have been painfully obtuse about what was going on with Lucy, but she didn't knowingly turn a blind eye. This revelation hits Maxine in the gut with far more force than the slap Lucy delivered last night.

Maxine needs to sit down, and she finds herself beside her mother on the couch. She knows that this relationship won't be fixed in one night, but she can't leave it this broken.

"Mom." Her mom turns to look at her, surprised to find her sitting so close. "I'm sorry I didn't call last night. You're right; it was thoughtless. Lucy any I weren't talking about you, we were just talking. Larry, he was a stupid prick and you deserved so much better. And Mom, I swear on Dad's grave I never said anything bad to him about you. I know Lucy didn't, either. I'm so sorry you believed that all these years."

Barb's eyes fill with tears, and at the same time, her face registers acute discomfort with this level of physical closeness and emotional candor. She nods, shrugs and turns back to the photo, and when Maxine takes her hand, she doesn't pull away but doesn't respond, either.

Maxine is suddenly overcome with fatigue, and she places her mom's hand back in her lap and rises. She goes upstairs to her childhood bedroom and climbs into bed. Within minutes, she is sound asleep.

Chloe waits nervously outside her parents' bedroom door, her wrapped birthday gifts for her father held clumsily in her arms. Her mom has gone in to see if he is awake and to bring him his breakfast. Chloe can't imagine how her dad can sleep for so long, and she wonders if he's faking it, like she did the day the police brought her home and her mom came up to her room. What if he just doesn't want to see her? Her mom has told her over and over that Gampa just died, that it was nobody's fault. But what if her dad thinks it was her fault?

The door opens and Chloe's mom comes out, but she closes the door behind her and Chloe's heart sinks. Then her mom squats down in front of her and smiles.

"Remember what we talked about? About how Daddy fell down and hurt his face?" she asks. Chloe nods somberly. "Well, I just want you to know what to expect. He doesn't look like himself. He has big bruises around both eyes, and his nose is puffy and a little crooked. Do you think that might scare you?"

Chloe shakes her head vehemently. "No, Mommy, I promise. He won't even know that I see it." Finally, a chance to give Daddy his presents! Chloe twitches with excitement and her mom smiles. She stands up and sighs.

"His mouth is a little swollen, too, so don't be surprised if he doesn't look as happy as you think he should. He really wants to see you and I know he'll love his gifts, but it's hard for him to smile properly. Okay?" Chloe's dark little head bobs up and down. "Okay. Let's go, then."

Her mom opens the door and motions for Chloe to go in first. Chloe takes a few scared steps, but when she sees her dad she breaks into a run. When she gets to the bed she drops the gifts on one corner and jumps up next to her dad. She can't believe how awful he looks close up, so she buries her face in his chest so he can't see her surprise. He laughs and drapes his arms around her.

"Hi there, my little cannoli. Whatcha got there?" His voice sounds funny and Chloe presses her face tighter against his chest. The bed shifts and Chloe sees out of the corner of one eye that her mom is sitting on the other side. Chloe starts to cry, because she doesn't want to look at him and she doesn't know what else to do. She's sure her mom will be mad.

"Hey, sweetie, it's just old Dad. What if you pretend I'm wearing a scary Halloween mask?"

Chloe looks up slowly, and as her dad wipes her tears she sees that it's not so bad, that it really is just Dad. After some quick thinking, she says, "Well, it's not a very good mask. I just missed you, that's all." She sits up and smiles, and sees her mom smile, too. She thinks her dad is smiling but isn't quite sure. "Do you want to open your presents now?"

Her father nods vigorously. "Absolutely. I've been waiting forever to see what you got me."

Chloe spins around and picks the biggest gift, a flat rectangle that she wrapped herself. She hands it to her father and watches as he tears the paper off slowly.

"A sketchpad. That sure is a lot of paper. What in the world am I going to do with all this paper?" he teases.

Chloe turns again and hands him a smaller present shaped like a long box. He unwraps this one, removes the cover and peers inside.

"Oh, of course, pencils! I can use these to draw on the paper, no?" Chloe giggles. "I was fresh out of paper *and* pencils. How did you know that?" Chloe shrugs. She hands him the last, much smaller, gift. He holds it to his ear and shakes it, then turns it over in his hands.

"Come on, Daddy!" Chloe bounces impatiently on the bed and her mom laughs.

Her dad finally pulls off the paper and finds a large eraser. "Oh, my, that's a fancy eraser. I can use this when I make mistakes, right?" Chloe nods happily.

Chloe's dad looks at her mom, who glances away. All of a sudden, Chloe feels like something's wrong, and not just Gampa dying or her dad hurting his face. Then her mom looks up and says brightly, "Don't forget the card, Chloe," and everyone seems okay again, but Chloe's not really sure what happened.

Her father opens the card and studies the front, which shows a man and a little girl holding hands and walking in a park. Chloe thought it was boring, but her mom said it was fine after their day of shopping at the big outdoor mall. Her dad flips it open and reads the greeting on the inside, which says, "Happy Birthday to the world's greatest dad!" Chloe thought that was stupid, too, so she had written, "Happy Birthday, Daddy. These are so you can keep drawing things you think are beautiful. Love, Chloe."

She asked her dad once when he was drawing how he decided what to draw and he said he drew what he found beautiful. After that, he did a sketch of her, and then one of her mom, too. Her mom framed them and hung them in their bedroom. He glances up at them now and then at her mom, and Chloe sees that he has tears in his eyes.

"Daddy?" Chloe whispers. He looks at her and pulls her into his arms and buries his bruised face in her hair. She mumbles into his shoulder, "Why are you sad?"

"I'm not sad, I'm happy. Thank you for the gifts, Chloe. They're perfect. And thank you for reminding me that I have everything I want right here." He pulls away and smiles, and at that moment, Chloe doesn't see the black eyes or the broken nose or the split lip. She just sees her father, happy.

Michael usually has a light schedule on Fridays, and it's just as well because he can't seem to stay focused. His next client isn't due for another forty-five minutes, so he takes two aspirin, sets the alarm on his watch and lies down on the couch usually occupied by his clients.

He spent a good deal of last night cleaning spots that the cleaning lady missed. He has told her numerous times that he is allergic to dust, but she rarely remembers to clean anything above eye level. As he dusted the tops of the refrigerator, cabinets, picture frames, window frames, the armoire and the top shelves of practically every closet, he again considered firing her, and again concluded he'd never find someone as cheap. Now he has a sinus headache and he's sure last night's cleaning is the cause.

He also has a stiff neck. Unable to spend another night alone in bed, he let himself fall asleep on the couch, and woke up sore and cranky. He wishes Maxine would remember that her home is here, with him, and realize that Astrid can take care of herself. So much time apart is forcing him to start asking some serious questions. Why haven't they set a wedding date? Why won't Maxine talk about having kids? Why is he in love with a woman with whom he has so little in common?

Last night he had a dream Maxine was giving him a blowjob, but when he looked down he realized it was Dr. Besser, instead. He woke up so aroused that he masturbated and came violently. He felt a bit guilty afterwards, even though he believes there's nothing wrong with fantasizing about other women. Now he imagines what it would be like to share his bed with Michelle, and this makes him wonder if it's Maxine he misses, or just having someone there. He'd pursued Maxine relentlessly, and never stopped to wonder if his goal was to spend the rest of his life with her or to simply win the chase.

He's tempted to dismiss these doubts as good old-fashioned cold feet, but that seems unoriginal, and the wedding isn't even on the horizon. It's natural to be attracted to other women even if one is in the securest relationship, of course. So why is he so troubled by Michelle's presence in Maxine's absence?

On a whim, Michael goes to his computer. He sends an instant message to Michelle to see if she is with a patient. She responds after a moment, "Nope. Come on in."

They discuss the events of Michael's last session with Sean. Michelle agrees that Sean is exhibiting classic symptoms of post traumatic stress disorder and that a reasonable period of treatment could be anywhere from six to twelve weeks, with ongoing follow up visits. She encourages Michael to consider a combination of cognitive behavioral therapy and medication, in addition to the play therapy and art therapy that he has tried unsuccessfully so far.

She's talking about the exciting research being done on pharmacologic interventions to treat PTSD in children and adolescents when Michael realizes that it's not cold feet he's experiencing. It's a simple compatibility issue. Michael considers his work the most important contribution he will make in his lifetime. Maxine is good at what she does, but she jumps from project to project, and to her, programming is just a way to make money. Maxine considers her work a job, and Michael thinks of his as a calling. He watches Dr. Besser now, reaching up to pull a psychiatric periodical from a shelf. She leans over her desk as she searches for an article, intensely focused, but smiling. Michael is impressed by her passion for her work and her commitment to helping others. From this angle, he can't help but appreciate her cleavage as well.

The alarm on Michael's watch beeps suddenly. Dr. Besser glances up.

Michael turns off the alarm and apologizes to Dr. Besser. "Sorry, I've got a client, but I think we're on the right track here. Let's pick this up later, okay?"

Dr. Besser nods. "No problem. I'll copy some articles for you to read." As Michael rises and walks to the door, he shoves his hands in his pants pockets to conceal his erection.

After a brief but excruciatingly painful trip to his doctor to have his nose straightened, Anthony sits in his car and checks for voice mails on his work line and his cell phone.

He figures if there's nothing that needs his immediate attention, he may as well go home for the day and take the weekend to let his wounds heal a bit before showing his face at the office. The only message at work is one of the partners offering his deepest sympathy and encouraging Anthony to take as much time as his family situation requires, as long as he's back for Monday's rescheduled meeting with the Seattle clients, who are eager to move forward.

On his cell phone is a message from Frank Elardi, left yesterday afternoon. "Just wondering what the fuck is going on, Tony. Let me know what you find out about your old man, or if there's anything else you want me to do." This call Anthony will have to return, but he decides to wait until he's home and has taken a couple of the Vicodin his doctor prescribed. Maybe then his brain will be more limber and he'll be able to come up with a plausible story.

When Anthony gets home, Sophie is sitting at the kitchen table. Before her on the table, seemingly forgotten, are a list of some sort, a pen and the telephone. She glances up as he enters, and two thoughts cross his mind: *God, she's beautiful. Something's wrong.*

"What did the doctor say?" she asks, but she's clearly distracted.

"Not to run into any more doors. What's the matter? What happened?" He doesn't remember any checkups scheduled with her doctor recently, but he's afraid she's gotten bad news about the cancer. He squats beside her and takes her hand.

"Deon's lawyer called. He wondered if it was necessary to have a restraining order. Oh, and he wanted to let us know Deon is filing a formal complaint with the police about that woman. He's tired of being roughed up, apparently."

Anthony sighs, relieved. "What did you tell him?"

"I told him to fuck off. Quel con. I said you're the one who should file a complaint." Sophie is quite pissed, but Anthony has a hard time keeping a straight face imagining some American lawyer being told off by his wisp of a French wife. If only the conversation had taken place in person, and Anthony could have witnessed it. That would have been the best birthday gift of all.

"Why are you laughing? What's funny?" Sophie demands, stamping her foot in distress.

Anthony pulls her to her feet and envelops her in a hug, lifting her off the floor. He laughs until it hurts his face too much, then sets her down and holds her face in his hands. He wants to kiss her but knows it will hurt like hell.

"I wish I could kiss you right now."

Sophie stands on her tiptoes and brushes his ruined lips with her own, light as a feather. It doesn't hurt a bit. Then she slaps his shoulder.

"Why do you laugh at me?" she asks again.

"I'm not laughing at you. I'm just happy to have you on my side." Sophie sighs and leans her forehead against his chest, and Anthony holds her until the throbbing in his nose reminds him of the prescription he had filled on his way home. He reaches into his pocket and pulls out the bottle of pills.

"What's this?" Sophie asks.

"Vicodin. At least I got some decent drugs out of the whole deal."

Anthony removes two pills and washes them down with a glass of water at the kitchen sink. Sophie sinks back onto the chair and shakes her head. "You'd be better off with a little wine or some brandy."

Anthony grins at her. "A little wine is what got me into this in the first place, no?"

Sophie protests, "A whole bottle on an empty stomach — "

"I know, baby, I'm kidding." Anthony sits next to her at the table. Suddenly, nothing seems funny anymore. He's glad Chloe doesn't know what happened, because he's so ashamed of his behavior, and of how poorly he interpreted his father's advice.

As if reading his mind, Sophie puts a hand on his arm and says, "You are a strong man, Anthony. Your father knew that. I know it, and Chloe knows it."

Anthony wants so much to believe her.

"Frank, it's Tony." Anthony is relieved to leave a message so he won't have to lie directly to Frank or answer any questions. "You know, I feel like a fucking idiot, but I've been so busy I completely forgot that my dad was traveling and letting a friend stay at his place. When he gets back from the homeland, I'll have him buy you a drink for your troubles. He'll get a kick out of this, I'm sure. Thanks for your help, man. I owe you."

Anthony hangs up abruptly and feels like a complete shit for dragging his old friend into this and then lying to him about it, especially since Frank's a cop. Last night Anthony dreamed of bloated bodies floating to the surface in a variety of locations, from the East River to Lake Washington. He knows he should probably contact the authorities, but he also wants to honor his father's wishes. He wouldn't have a clue whom to contact, anyway. He certainly doesn't want to get Frank any more involved than he already is, and so he decides the best course of action right now is to do nothing. The Vicodin has kicked in, and Anthony drops the phone on the bed next to him and slides under the covers. Times like these, he wishes he went to church and had a priest to consult, but what would he say? *Forgive me Father for I have sinned. It's been nineteen years since my last confession. My father jumped off the Brooklyn Bridge and I lied about it to a buddy of mine. Do you think I should tell someone?* Then Anthony remembers suicide is a mortal sin and a priest is the last person he should tell. If anyone belongs in heaven, it's his dad. Anthony doesn't know whom he can trust. That old fart Father Grimaldi never seemed trustworthy. Is he the enemy? Unwillingly, Anthony slips back into his world of good guys and bad guys, battles and corpses.

As Maxine heads out of town to see Mr. Retter's new house, she tells herself that there is nothing weird about this. She and Mr. Retter — Jay — have kept in touch over the years, enough so that she considers him a friend. She used to drop in on him at school when she was home visiting, and several times they've run into each other in town and had coffee, or lunch. Sure, they have a certain easy connection, more of a chemistry, really, but most likely the physical attraction is all in her head, and that's where it will stay. As she turns into his winding driveway, she vows that she will do nothing to ruin their friendship, or worse, make an ass of herself.

The house is all angles and glass, but the materials and colors allow it to blend effortlessly into its wooded setting. The siding is dark taupe, like weathered cedar, and the trim is forest green. As she rolls to a stop before the porch, Maxine observes a striking copper awning that tops the front door, which is also painted green. It's beautiful, and Maxine can't imagine to what her mother objects, other than the fact that it doesn't look like her own house.

As Maxine climbs out of the car and approaches the house, the front door swings open and Mr. Retter — *Jay, Jay, Jay, you idiot* — stands under the awning, smiling. He's wearing an old concert T-shirt and jeans, and is barefoot. Maxine thought about changing her clothes before leaving, and now she's glad she didn't fall prey to her own vanity. She did shave her legs and put on nice underwear, of course. She isn't a savage, for Christ's sake.

Maxine jokes, "Thank God my mom talked me out of that strapless number I had on." Jay chuckles. She hops up the few steps to the porch and says, "Hi there. Thanks for the book."

"Hi. You're welcome." He steps inside. "And welcome."

Maxine follows him inside and is struck by how familiar the inside of the house feels, at least what she can see of it. A small entryway leads into an open great room. The kitchen is to the left, the dining area is tucked in the corner and the living room is straight ahead. The entire back wall is floor to ceiling windows and sliding doors that open onto a back deck. At the right end of the living area, a huge stone fireplace divides this space from whatever lies beyond, and a hallway that Maxine suspects leads to bedrooms and bathrooms. Exposed beams and vaulted tongue in groove ceilings give the interior a warm, earthy feel. It's on the smaller side, like Astrid's and John's house, with the same efficient use of space. The furniture is big and inviting, but the room doesn't feel crowded.

"Can I get you a drink? I've got beer and wine, but not much of a bar."

Maxine stops gawking and sees that Jay is in the kitchen standing in front of the open refrigerator with a bottle of beer in his hand. He takes a swig. She wonders what kind of wine he has, but changes her mind. "Whatever you're having is fine."

Maxine is drawn into the living room toward the expanse of glass. Jay joins her and hands her a beer. She smiles and says, "My mom was right, this is just awful. What were you thinking?" She takes a sip of cold beer.

Grinning, Jay reaches out, opens a sliding door and steps out onto the deck. He leaves the door open and goes to check on something cooking in a large grill off to the left. Maxine steps out and smells something delicious as a puff of smoke drifts her way. She realizes that the deck stretches the entire length of the back of the house. Then she notices the view.

Maxine steps to the railing and murmurs, "Holy shit." The house is built on a hill, and beyond a small stretch of level ground, the terrain drops away to a huge wooded ravine. The deck is elevated, however, so that even the little back yard is far below. Maxine sees some lawn furniture and a shed, and minimal but tasteful, low-maintenance landscaping.

"Yeah, it's the best I could do on a teacher's salary." Jay is at her side, leaning on the railing, and Maxine peers at him in profile as he surveys his little slice of the world. She takes a long swig of beer, and then realizes she's forgotten something.

"Oh, wait, I've got a bottle of champagne in the car! I totally forgot about it, trying to follow those crazy directions you gave me. I'll just be a second." She turns, but Jay puts a hand on her arm.

"Too late, dinner's ready. You can get it later."

Maxine hesitates, enjoying his hand warming her arm, then nods. She notices a round outdoor dining table not far from the grill, set casually for dinner and loaded with food. As they settle in, Maxine raises her beer.

"To your new home. It's spectacular, really." Jay touches his bottle to hers.

"Thank you. I'm glad you could be here."

They help themselves to grilled steaks, vegetables and foil wrapped baked potatoes. There seems to be an enormous amount of food on the table.

"Um, are you expecting the swim team? Some kind of book club meeting?

Jay laughs. "I always make way more than I can eat so I'll have leftovers for the week. Lazy divorced guys' secret weapon."

Maxine can't come up with a response to the divorce remark, so she says, "If I move back here I'll be tipping the scales at two hundred before long. I've done nothing but eat since I got here. I feel like a fatted calf."

Maxine thinks she sees Jay's gaze pass over her ring finger. The diamond is hard to miss. Michael made sure of that.

"Are you sure you've had enough? I mean, don't worry about me next week, I'll get by somehow if you're still hungry."

Maxine laughs. "Nice. Seriously, that was delicious." She leans back in her chair, her hands on her full tummy, her eyes closed. "Give me five minutes and I'll spring into action and clean up this carnage." Maxine sighs contentedly. They've had a fun dinner, gossiping mostly about mutual acquaintances and catching up on their own lives, avoiding the subjects of divorce and engagement.

"I've got a better idea. Why don't we take a walk, work off a little dinner and then grab that bottle of champagne from your car?"

Maxine opens one eye and trains it on Jay. "You can't be serious."

Jay rises and picks up both of their half full beers. "Come on, you have to tour the grounds before you go."

Maxine makes a production of heaving herself to her feet, with the words "before you go" ringing in her ears. She doesn't want to go, so any activity that will postpone her departure seems like a good idea. She takes her beer from Jay and follows him back through the house. They exit the front door, descend the porch steps and turn right, and as they round the corner, Maxine notices a garage at the kitchen end of the house. As they continue past the garage, she sees an expanse of flagstone steps leading down to the back yard.

"If we go down these steps, you do realize we'll have to climb back up them, yes?" Maxine queries with some concern.

"Hold onto the railing. They can be a little uneven." Jay starts down the steps, still barefoot, and Maxine has little choice but to follow. The sun has set but there's still plenty of light to navigate the steep path. There's a hint of a chill in the air, and Maxine breathes in deeply, surprised at how much she has missed this heady aroma of summer blooms, forest, earth and chimney smoke.

"Why does it always smell so good here?" she wonders.

"Because it's home," Jay replies.

Once they've toured the lower property and conquered the return ascent in the rapidly fading light, Maxine retrieves the champagne from her car and follows Jay into the house, trying not to appear winded. She must admit she has more energy than she did after dinner, having shed that overfull feeling as she trailed Jay up the steps, admiring his posterior most of the way. Jay pulls two champagne flutes from a cabinet while Maxine opens the bottle, holding a kitchen towel over the cork to avoid launching it into any of the recessed lights in the kitchen. After a muffled "pop," she fills the glasses as Jay holds them aloft.

She raises hers to make a toast, but Jay motions to the deck and they step out into the darkness. Without prompting, Maxine looks up. Above them, millions of stars begin their nightly show. It's breathtaking.

"To home," Jay says beside her.

"To home." Maxine touches her glass to his and they both sip. Maxine shivers, partly from the chill but mostly due to the perfection of the moment. She crosses her arms and leans on the railing.

"You're cold. Should we go inside?" he asks.

"No."

Jay moves behind her and puts a hand on either side of her on the railing, as if to warm her. His arms are long enough that he doesn't touch her, but Maxine feels a tingling sensation the length of her spine. She knows all she needs to do is back up an inch or so, or simply turn around. But she doesn't. She won't be the one to make the first move. She realizes just how tired she is of being in control, of performing sexually rather than making love. The weariness washes over her and leaves her frustrated, and a little angry.

"I should go before I get drunk and can't find my way home," she says lightly, pressing as close to the railing as possible. She feels physical pain once the words are out, because she wants more than anything to stay.

Jay backs away slowly. She expects him to become aloof, but he surprises her by protesting, "But you haven't seen the best part of the house." She turns to find him smiling down at her. He takes her glass from her. "No more of this, though." He sets both glasses on the railing and takes her hand, leading her toward another set of glass doors. He slides one open and stands back so she can enter.

The room is dark and Maxine waits just inside until Jay switches on a lamp. As her eyes adjust to the light, she gasps. She stands with a hand over her mouth, taking it all in. Behind her is the wall of glass. On her right is the other side of the stone fireplace. In front of the fireplace are two leather club chairs, each with its own reading lamp and side table, and a big, square, leather ottoman in front of them. Covering the other two walls are floor to ceiling shelves, filled with nothing but books. There is even a library ladder. A thick rug covers the wood floor and gives the room a rich, hushed feel. Maxine walks over to one wall and runs her fingers gently along the book spines, tilting her head to read the authors and titles. When she reaches the ladder, she gives it a little push and it glides smoothly along its track. She hears Jay chuckle behind her.

Maxine turns slowly in a complete circle, and stops when she once again faces Jay. "It's the perfect room," she whispers.

"You don't have to whisper," he whispers. "It's not a real library."

"But it's fantastic," Maxine protests. "I can't believe you didn't show it to me right away."

"Well, I know about your problem with books and I didn't want to torture you. But I couldn't resist. Sorry." He is self-conscious, embarrassed by his obvious pride.

Maxine continues her inspection of the volumes, completely lost in a world in which she feels right at home.

"What have you been reading?" She's so engrossed that she turns with a start, as if surprised to find him still standing there.

"DHARMA GIRL, by Chelsea Cain. She's a Portland author. I just finished it, actually. It's really good."

He nods. "What's it about?"

Maxine stares at Jay and thinks about this carefully before responding, "It's about going home."

Jay walks slowly over to Maxine and stands close. He lifts her left hand, studying the ring. "Are you going to marry him?"

Maxine can hardly breathe. She stares at her hand in his, then looks up at this man she has fantasized about for so long. What began as a schoolgirl crush has grown into something more over the years. She knows what she's giving up, and has no idea what she's heading into, but before she can change her mind she shakes her head slowly and says, "No."

He pulls her into his arms, hard. She wraps her arms around his waist and turns her head to one side, listening to his heart beating. He strokes her hair, then pulls her head back. He kisses her in a way she has always wanted to be kissed, as if he needs her mouth more than air, as if he might devour her. He presses his entire body against hers.

He leads her to the ottoman and lays her down, her legs dangling from the knees over the edge. He stands before her and takes off his shirt, then his jeans. He wears boxer briefs, and the sight of his body, the fact that he undressed first, the way he looks at her, arouse Maxine so much she squirms impatiently.

He bends over her and kisses her softly, running a hand down her body, his mouth trailing after, brushing a breast, pulling up her shirt to kiss her stomach, then slowly unzipping her pants and pulling them off. He leans over her again, stroking her inner thigh and between her legs, watching her face as she reacts. He kisses her roughly and she can feel his erection against her leg, but when she reaches to touch him he grabs her hand, then the other, and pulls her to a sitting position. He kneels and pulls her shirt over her head, then kisses her again, removing her bra, his hands on her breasts, pulling her body against his, skin on skin. Then he pushes her back down on the ottoman and takes off her panties.

Maxine cries out when his mouth touches her, and she turns her head to the side and sees their reflection in the glass, his head between her thighs and his hands pushing her knees farther apart, opening her up. She tries to distance herself somehow, to handle the intensity by watching the scene as a third party, but it's still too much. She grasps at him and tries to pull him to her, but he continues exploring her with his mouth and his fingers until she begs, "Please, please, please." Then she is being lifted off the ottoman and deposited on the rug, and he's on top of her, inside her. He presses her hands on either side of her head, and she's no longer worried about who is or isn't in control.

Maxine stops thinking and closes her eyes. When he's ready to let her come he kisses her gently and whispers, "Hey," so she opens her eyes and stares into his as they come together.

Maxine likes that he doesn't pull away, but stays on top of her, their bodies entangled, breathing heavily into each other's necks, until he eventually slips out of her. He props himself on an elbow and smiles down at her, brushing away the sweaty hair stuck to her face. He presses his lips to her forehead, and then kisses her mouth softly before rolling onto his back. They catch their breath.

"You give a really thorough house tour, Mr. Retter," Maxine says finally, pulling her knees together.

"Mmmm. It was the ladder that did it, wasn't it?" He stretches out a long, sinewy leg and sends the ladder gliding. "It works every time." He finds her hand and squeezes it, as if to make sure she knows he's joking.

"Definitely the ladder." Maxine turns her head and studies his body next to hers. She shivers, thinking about all the times she imagined being naked with him, and how reality is so much better than anything she expected.

He turns and looks at her, then brings her hand to his mouth and kisses it. "It's chilly, isn't it? How about a fire and a blanket, maybe some champagne?" She nods, and he sits up, but is distracted by the sight of her. He traces a path from her hair all the way down to her toes, taking his time around her clavicle and hipbones.

Turned on again by his gaze and his touch, Maxine warns, "Don't start something you can't finish, old man." He laughs and gets up. As he steps out the open door, he turns.

"Will you stay?" he asks, an afterthought.

Maxine nods, but then adds, "I'll just have to, you know, call my mom."

CHAPTER TEN

Anthony is up with the sun, tired of thrashing in bed, dreaming of war and death and betrayal. His father's words, "They need you to be a strong man," continue to haunt him, but he's sure that spending days in bed is not what his hard-working father had in mind. So he resorts to the first stereotypical family-man activity that comes to mind: yard work.

Trees, shrubs and ground cover can get out of hand quickly in this fertile climate, so Sophie chose slow growing species when she designed and planted their yard. Anthony once again appreciates her foresight when he sees how little pruning is necessary. In a few hours, he has thinned, shaped and cut back what was overgrown, and bagged the debris for recycling. There is a patch of grass in the back yard for Chloe, and it's about a foot tall. Since it's still wet with dew and far too much for the reel mower to handle, Anthony decides to wait until a decent hour to subject the neighbors to the power mower.

Sophie's single whimsy was the wisteria arbor. They saw one in full bloom in the Japanese Garden in

Portland, and agreed it would be worth the maintenance. At first, Anthony found it bothersome. Now it's actually intimidating. It never stops growing. Its shoots wrap themselves around the patio furniture if left unchecked. Anthony imagines he could sit down with a cooler of beer and watch the vines encircle him if he had the time and inclination to be strangled in his own back yard. Furthermore, they endured three years of frustration waiting for the diva to bloom. The fourth year, she graced them with six flowers. The following year, they were rewarded for their patience, and enjoyed a spectacular show of huge, dangling, purple blossoms. Brief, but worth the wait.

This year's performance has long since passed, and Anthony has yet to address the tangled mass of vines stretching outward, seeking hold of anything within reach. He'll have to remove the robins' nest, too, which he has been meaning to do since Chloe determined it was officially abandoned. They explained to Chloe that the nest had to come down because it might attract bugs, and they don't want the mama robin to take up residence in the same treacherous spot next year.

Usually, Anthony resigns himself to spending at least two hours cutting back unwanted shoots and redirecting the keepers, but once he gets started, he'll find himself engrossed in the challenge. He enjoys crafting an aesthetically pleasing and architecturally tasteful design from flora, a largely unfamiliar medium to him.

Today, however, once Anthony drags out the ladder and starts clipping away, the sheer number of branches twisting this way and that overcomes him. They seem to come at him from every direction. For each shoot he snips, for every vine he twists in the desired direction, half a dozen more appear, and repeatedly he climbs down the ladder to check his progress from a distance, keeping his eye on the big picture. Once he's back up among the tangled vines, however, he loses perspective and worries that he'll cut what should be kept or keep what should be cut. He decides to wait for Sophie's help before he does irreversible damage.

He turns his attention to the empty robin's nest in the corner. He studies it with admiration, impressed with the resourcefulness of the robins that built it. Along with twigs, grass, feathers and leaves is an assortment of yarn, shredded paper and what appears to be some kind of animal fur. All of it is bound tightly together, and as precarious as it appeared from below, it is firmly embedded among the beams of the arbor and the main trunk of the wisteria. Anthony's first attempts to dislodge it while keeping it intact are in vain, and he wonders which garden tools would be best suited for dismantling it.

"What are you doing, Daddy?" Chloe demands from below. Anthony peers down and finds Sophie and Chloe watching him from the patio. They are both dressed, and Sophie sips a mug of coffee. He was so focused on his project that he didn't hear them come out and has no idea why they're up at this hour.

"I'm taking down the nest, pumpkin. We talked about this, remember? What are you doing up, anyway?"

Chloe stamps her foot impatiently, as if he's teasing her, and says, "It's Saturday, Daddy! We're going to be late!" She looks to her mom for confirmation, and Sophie nods, then looks up at Anthony.

"How long have you been up?" Sophie asks.

"Uh, a while I guess." Sophie glances around the tidy yard and raises an eyebrow. Anthony has completely lost track of time, and he realizes that it is Saturday and Chloe is talking about the farmers market.

"Chloe, run inside and bring your dad a coffee, okay?" Sophie says quietly.

Once she's out of earshot, Sophie says, "Would you prefer we go on without you? You could finish what you've started and join us for breakfast, no?"

Anthony sometimes suspects Sophie can read his mind. This morning's physical and mental exertion is therapeutic and is providing a much-needed sense of accomplishment, and he doesn't want to drop everything when he's so close to finishing. "What about Chloe?"

"I'll tell her I asked you to finish your work so I can have her all to myself." Sophie is an expert at little white lies. Anthony sometimes wonders how many fibs he's fallen for over the years, and if they're all as innocent as this one.

He nods. "Okay." Chloe reappears with a cup of coffee and hands it to Sophie, who sets in on a step of the ladder.

"Okay what? Are you ready?" Chloe asks.

"Your father's trying to keep the nest in one piece so we can see it when we get home. Seulement les filles cette fois, oui?" Sophie shepherds Chloe back into the house and leaves Anthony to the renewed challenge of removing the nest without destroying it. He picks up his coffee as he descends the ladder and sips it on his way to the shed to look for the proper tools. He's grateful for Sophie's understanding, but the minute they're gone, he misses them. Lately, no matter how much stronger and healthier Sophie appears, he hates the thought of his girls out in the world without him.

Chloe is mad. Now that her mom can finally go to the market, her dad stays home. One week. That's all she got with both of them on her favorite day.

"Why can't Daddy just come with us and do the nest later? All he does is sleep, and now he can't go to the market because of some stupid bird nest?"

Her mom turns and says sharply, "Chloe!"

Chloe feels the sting of tears in her eyes and turns to look out the window. Her mother hasn't spoken harshly to her in months and it makes her feel strange, sad and mad at the same time. They ride in silence.

Finally, her mother says, "Je suis désolé, ma petite. I asked him to stay. I've missed being just with you. Should we go back and get him?" She pulls the car to the side of the road and stops.

Chloe feels even worse now, but doesn't want her mom to see it. She shrugs and continues staring out the window.

"Chloe, look at me," her mom implores. Chloe tries to make her face look mad and turns to her mom. Right away, she's sorry for acting like such a brat because her mom looks so upset.

"Are you scared to go to the market with just me? I know I got tired and grumpy at the mall the other day, but we did so much walking."

Chloe knows she'll cry if she tries to talk, so she just shakes her head.

"Are you sure? If you want Daddy to come with us, it won't hurt my feelings, I promise." Her mom smiles.

Chloe thinks she's already hurt her feelings. "I'm sure, Mommy," she whispers. "Like you said, just us girls this time."

It's weird being alone at the market with her mom, but not because Chloe is nervous. Her mom acts different. She's chattier with the vendors and takes her time picking what she wants. A lot of the vendors are men, and they act different, too, without her father there. Plus, her mom isn't paying as much attention to Chloe as she would like, which makes her wonder why she wanted to be alone with her. She seems happy, though, and Chloe thinks maybe it has something to do with how the men look at her the way they used to, before she got sick.

Maxine makes small talk with her mother while waiting for Lucy to pick her up. Her mom is subdued this morning, not surprising considering how tanked she sounded last night when Maxine called to tell her she'd be spending the night with a friend. She was still in bed when Maxine got home, and by the time Maxine was packed and ready to go she figured she shouldn't leave without saying good bye. Now they sit at the kitchen table nibbling on donuts and sipping coffee.

Maxine is determined to make these last few moments with her mother count. This is unfamiliar terrain, as she usually strives to get in and out of these visits with as little real interaction as possible. But Maxine started something she didn't have time to finish yesterday afternoon, and despite the fact that she won't find closure today, she yearns for the briefest connection. She takes a gulp of coffee that burns her throat and dives in.

"Lucy asked me about Dad the other night. It was weird, but I really had to think about it to come up with something specific. You know what I remembered?"

Her mom looks at her as if she's not quite sure she heard her correctly. She shakes her head slowly from side to side with a look of dread. Maxine wonders if this is a bad idea, but figures she doesn't have much to lose where her relationship with her mom is concerned.

"I remembered how every night, when he came home from work, he'd hug you and lift you off the floor. Then he'd pick me up and dance me around the room." Maxine trails off. Her mother stares at her but doesn't say anything. Maxine jumps up and goes to the living room to retrieve the old family photo.

She sits back down next to her mom and holds the picture between them. "I love this picture. You look beautiful. And we were all happy, weren't we?"

Maxine's mother takes the photo from Maxine, lays it face down on the table and shakes her head. "Don't. Please." Her eyes fill with tears.

"Okay," Maxine replies, "no trip down memory lane. No what ifs. But I need to ask you something. You really loved Daddy, didn't you?" Her mom nods. Maxine continues, "How did you know? How did you know it was real?"

Barb straightens, wipes her eyes and takes a deep breath, considering her reply carefully. "I felt safe with him. I knew he would always come home and hug me and I would feel safe." She shrugs as if this is inadequate, but it is exactly what Maxine needs to hear. If only her mother could be inside her head at this moment, she might also experience the feeling of a window being opened in her brain, letting out the stale, smoky air of uncertainty that was trapped for so long.

A horn sounds outside. Maxine knows Lucy won't come in. "That's Lucy." Maxine stands to pick up her overnight bag, then bends and wraps an arm around her mom's neck. Into her hair she whispers, "Thank you. I love you, Mom." At the door she turns to see her mother staring after her with a curious, sad smile.

"I can't believe this. You slept with Jay Retter." On the way to the airport, Lucy is beside herself. "I knew you would. He's old! What was it like? You have to tell me everything. I knew it. I totally knew it."

Maxine feigns offense. "Please. You didn't know anything. I didn't plan it, it just happened. And stop calling him old."

"Did you shave your legs?" Lucy demands.

"Yes, but I tend to do that when they're hairy."

"Did you do it in the morning when you showered at my house or later at mom's?"

Maxine looks out the window.

"What color underwear were you wearing? Black?"

Again, no answer.

"Okay, sister, spill it or I'm pulling over right now. Was it good?"

Maxine sighs. "It may have been the best night of my life, so far anyway."

Lucy almost swerves off the road. Her voice softens. "Oh my God, Maxine. You really dig him, don't you?"

Maxine's cell phone rang early this morning, before eight o'clock. Detective Hancock informed her apologetically that the district attorney was moving forward with assault charges and that it would be in her best interest to return to Kirkland, pronto. She padded from the living room, where she'd found her phone, into Jay's bedroom. Standing at the foot of his bed naked, she told him he was harboring a fugitive. She had told him the entire gruesome story last night, so he wasn't caught off guard. He climbed out of bed and wrapped her in a hug so warm and comforting and safe that she almost believed if she stayed there in his arms, nothing could harm her.

Lucy gives her Valium for the flight, but Maxine doesn't take them when she gets to her gate, or when she boards the plane. She wants to be alert these last hours before she gets to Kirkland. She wants to be alert so she can relive every moment of last night and this morning.

Maxine can't remember the last time she was with a man simply to be close to him, as close as she could get without crawling under his skin. She spent the better part of last night exploring every inch of Jay's body, trying to memorize him, so that when they were apart she could recall the feel of his skin, his smell and his taste, the way he looked at her when he was inside her, how he said her name. It was as if she knew what awaited her, and that it might be a while before she saw him again and she would need these reserves of memories on which to draw. She is physically exhausted from a night of talking and touching and storing information in her brain, but she remains awake the entire flight, mentally cataloging each kiss, caress, whisper, laugh. His last words to her were, "If you need me, I'll be there in a heartbeat."

On the drive home, Maxine makes no pretense with Michael. They share a perfunctory hug at the curb when he picks her up, but other than banal conversation about the weather in Kirkland versus Bozeman, neither of them tries to reconnect. Maxine has a fleeting awareness that Michael is oddly distant, but assumes it's a reaction to her own moody behavior and the circumstances of her homecoming. He warned her that this was a bad time to leave, and he is surely pleased to be right.

At home, Maxine brings her bag upstairs and stands in the center of their bedroom, unsure how to proceed. Michael said something about being in the office and told her to let him know when she was ready to go to the station. Maxine thinks he should have just said, "when you're ready to turn yourself in," because that's obviously what he was thinking. She brings her bag into the closet and notices idly that Michael has tidied her clothing in her absence. She wonders whether she should unpack or pack. There seems to be no point in putting away her things in this place that has never felt, nor will ever feel, like home. Alone and uncertain, she flips open her cell and finds Detective Hancock's number.

"Hi, it's Maxine Reise. I'm here. What's the drill?"

Turning oneself in to be placed under arrest is mostly tedious, Maxine concludes. She and Michael meet her defense lawyer at the station. Once she has brought him up to speed on the incident, Thomas ("call me Tom") Kerin, to whom Michael was referred by a colleague, lets Maxine know what to expect today. Michael waits while Tom accompanies Maxine through booking, fingerprinting and, by far the most embarrassing, photographing. The process takes longer than she imagined, but everyone is professional and friendly, although they seem to view her as somewhat of a curiosity. Detective Hancock makes an appearance for some paperwork and he and Maxine exchange hellos. She can tell that he feels sorry for her and she wonders why.

Tom leaves Maxine alone in an interview room while he goes to confer with the ADA, or assistant district attorney. Maxine has watched enough television to feel slightly offended that he felt the need to clarify "ADA." He's a nice guy, though, and Maxine is comforted by his avuncular nature and thirty-plus years of experience.

Once she's been alone for ten or fifteen minutes, the haze of fatigue and denial that allowed her to remain relatively calm and detached until now begins to evaporate. When Tom asked her if she had any questions before they began she just shook her head, as if this was something she did every day. What she didn't ask then but would very much like to ask now is, *"Am I going to spend even one minute in a jail cell?"*

She takes a few deep breaths with her hands to her face, then pulls a section of her hair to her nose and inhales. She and Jay took a shower together this morning before she drove to her mom's house, and her skin and hair still smell of his soap and shampoo. It's his smell, or rather, his smell when he's clean and hasn't been screwing her for hours. She wishes she hadn't showered at all, because then she'd be able to smell *him* right now instead of his soap, but this is better than nothing.

The door swings open and Tom strides into the room looking pleased with himself. He sits across from her. "Good news and bad news, kiddo. You can leave as soon as I'm done with you. This is a weak case and the ADA knows it. She's charging you with simple assault, but as a felony instead of a misdemeanor. You acted in self-defense and with no malicious intent, yada yada yada. The only wrinkle is that you took the child, which could technically be considered kidnapping — "

"Chloe," Maxine interrupts. Tom peers at her, puzzled. "The little girl. Her name is Chloe."

"Okay, you took Chloe with you, but you called the police right away and cooperated fully, so kidnapping is a big stretch. But since there's a child involved, the DA wants to cover all his bases, according to the ADA. She's agreed to release you OR — on your own recognizance."

Maxine is so tense that she's kept perfectly still for fear that her rigid muscles might creak if called into service. With this bit of news, however, her body goes slack and she almost slides out of her chair. Tom looks slightly alarmed.

"What about bail?" Maxine asks weakly.

"No bail. Just show up for your arraignment hearing in two days. If you don't show up, then you're in real trouble, young lady." Tom chuckles. "You'll enter a plea of not guilty, the judge will set a date for your pre-trial hearing, and you'll be out of there before you know it. Okay? Okay. Let's get you home, then."

Michael drops Maxine at home and tells her he needs to swing by his office to do a little research. Truth be told, he needs time alone to process the fact that his fiancée was just booked on felony assault. Furthermore, she's behaving like a child who may be suspended for fighting on the playground, her only defense, "He started it!" Equally irksome is how everyone, from the defense lawyer to Detective Hancock, is handling her with kid gloves, as if she's some sort of martyr. Michael wants to be supportive and help her through this, but he has issues with Maxine's attitude and, frankly, it bothers him that she hasn't even acknowledged that her legal troubles could affect his practice. By the time he sits down at his desk and turns on his computer, he's quite pissed, and believes he made a wise decision to put some space between them right now.

Michelle left Michael copies of several research articles on treating children like Sean with medication, and he skims them idly. Personally, he thinks it's premature and that most psychiatrists are too quick to medicate, particularly where kids are concerned. Yet he's willing to keep an open mind.

A blinking light on his phone alerts him to new voicemails, and he keys in his password to see if anything can't wait until Monday. There is one message from a client needing to schedule an appointment, which he skips, but the next one commands his full attention.

"Hi, it's Michelle. I hope you check your voicemail on weekends, because I don't have your cell or home phone numbers. Anyway, listen, I don't normally mix business with pleasure, but you mentioned that you haven't made many social connections since you moved here, and I know this is late notice, but I'm having a little barbeque tomorrow — Sunday — afternoon, and thought it might be fun for you to meet some of my friends. Totally casual, no need to bring anything. Around three. I left my address on your desk. Hope to see you there!"

Michael pushes a button and replays the message, listening to it again as he searches his desk for her address, which he finds on a little card in his "IN" box. He smiles at the sound of her voice and how she seems a little flustered. He notes that she lives in quite a hip neighborhood.

This is one work function he won't try to persuade Maxine to attend. His mood greatly improved, he delves back into the research articles with renewed interest.

"This must be getting old, huh? Enough about me, let's talk some more about me."

Maxine and Father Brian are having dinner at a restaurant in Seattle away from the school, mostly because it's a Saturday night and Maxine wanted to avoid the younger crowd closer to campus. Also, Brian was bored and felt like exploring the city. Maxine picked a cheap Thai place she knows Michael would hate, but that Brian loves, if the number of dishes he ordered and is consuming with gusto is any indication. She remains fascinated and quite envious of his metabolism.

Brian juts out his lower jaw and brushes his chin with his fingers. "Someday — and that day may never come — I'll call upon you to do a service for me."

Maxine rolls her eyes. "That is easily the worst Godfather impression I have ever heard." Brian looks wounded. She stabs at her own green papaya salad, which is delicious but undeniably on the light and healthy side. She ordered it with the specific goal of losing the pounds she'd put on in Bozeman, so the next time she is naked with Jay, if there is a next time in the near future, she might be down to her usual weight. Having such an impure thought in front of a priest made her blush.

"I can't believe they arrested you. I'm sorry, Maxine. You don't deserve this." Brian spears a prawn and studies it briefly before popping it in his mouth.

"I'm freaked about the arrest and everything, but my lawyer doesn't seem to think there's much chance the charges will, you know, stick." She feels odd saying this, as if she's imitating a character on a crime drama who routinely uses words like "perp" and "shooter."

"Thank God. I can't really picture you behind bars. So what's really bugging you?"

Maxine takes a gigantic bite and chews as she considers her reply. Finally, she swallows and says, "I feel like I messed up royally and I should apologize." Brian nods. "My lawyer would have a heart attack if he heard me say that."

"Who do you believe deserves an apology?" Brian asks.

"That's the thing — I don't know. Half the time I think I should apologize to Michael for being such a pain in the ass." She's still perplexed by Michael's behavior when he came home this afternoon. He was buoyant but oddly distant, as if he was high or something.

"What about the man you kicked?" Brian asks.

"No." The immediacy of Maxine's response surprises her. "That's weird, isn't it?"

Brian shrugs. "Who else comes to mind?"

Maxine pushes the food around on her plate. She knows the answer but can't imagine saying it aloud. Finally, she sighs and looks up. "The little girl, Chloe, and her parents. They must be suffering more than anyone, and I just want them to know that I really thought I was doing the right thing. But is that selfish? I mean, it can't really help them now."

Brian thinks this over. "I don't think it's selfish to admit that you could have made a mistake. And maybe it would help them to see you as a person who is suffering, too. To know that you aren't taking this lightly, which obviously you're not. The legal side of it, I can't help you with. But giving this family the gift of your honesty and empathy, I think that might bring all of you some peace. Does it feel right to you?"

Maxine says, "If you're telling me to trust my instincts, that's what got me into this mess in the first place." Brian smiles sympathetically. "Okay, enough. What's up with you?"

Brian smiles innocently. "Well, you know I constantly have my ear to the ground where all things Bozeman are concerned." Maxine nods, expecting some juicy gossip. "Violet, the woman who owns Turn the Page, has always been particularly eager to keep me abreast of what's going on in town." Maxine groans, dreading what's coming. Turn the Page is Lucy's bookstore, of course. Brian continues, "She emailed me today that Jay Retter bought a book yesterday for the manager's sister after a long tête-à-tête in the literature section. Have you anything to confess, my child?"

Maxine again finds herself pushing a stranger's doorbell, this time with a steady hand and even steadier resolve. She recalled Chloe's address easily from the day the police came to drive her home, and had no trouble finding the lovely house, not far from her own but on a street with a completely different feel to it. She imagines the people who live in these houses know each other, that their kids go to school together and they have block parties in the summers. It's still light enough out that there are kids playing in their yards and in the street.

The door opens and a petite woman with a French accent asks curiously, "May I help you?" Maxine's first thought is that she is clearly at the right address because this woman looks just like Chloe. Her second thought is that Chloe's dark eyes, which struck her as so troubled, were inherited from her mother.

"Mrs. Scialfa? I'm so sorry to bother you. I'm Maxine Reise." The woman tilts her head and Maxine realizes there is no reason her name should be familiar. "I took your daughter, Chloe, from the house on Fuller." The woman's eyebrows, or what is left of them, shoot up. Belatedly, Maxine sees that Chloe's mom isn't just petite but thin, and that her head is covered with a silk scarf for reasons other than fashion. She is ill. She is ill and having to deal with the mess that Maxine created, all because her daughter's dark eyes reminded her of Lucy's.

"Please, give me just a minute. I know I'm probably the last person you want to see right now, but — "

Just then, the sound of footsteps causes Maxine to look past Chloe's mom into the house. She freezes at the sight of Chloe, beyond the front living room and down a short hallway.

Chloe, however, lights up. Her face breaks into a smile and she runs toward them. "Maxine!" she cries breathlessly, but stops suddenly a few feet away when her mother turns sharply to stare at her.

There is a moment of confusion that Maxine can't understand right now. Chloe's mother looks stunned by Chloe's excitement. Chloe, registering this, immediately stops looking excited and ducks behind her mom, peeking out at Maxine. Maxine wants to say something to her, but doesn't want to step on any toes, and so she smiles but says nothing. There is a heavy silence until Chloe's mom murmurs something quietly in French that Maxine doesn't understand but that sends Chloe scurrying back down the hall and out of sight.

"I'm so sorry. I shouldn't have come here. I don't know what I was thinking — "

Chloe's mother reaches out suddenly and takes Maxine's arm, pulling her into the house. They stand there in the little entry for a moment, the family room to the right. Maxine can't help but notice that this house has that unique European style that is neither overly designed nor deliberately decorated, but is simply furnished so personally and beautifully that it feels like a home. She thinks of Astrid, and Lucy, and Jay, and this causes her such acute longing that tears blur her vision.

"Tell me then," Chloe's mother says. "Why are you here?"

Maxine doesn't hesitate. "I made a mistake. I thought I saw something that wasn't there and I reacted without thinking. I'm so sorry. I'm sorry for all the pain this must have caused your family, especially Chloe. But I swear to you, I thought I was doing the right thing at the time." Maxine's voice catches and she stops talking abruptly, trying to stop the tears.

"Maxine?" Maxine nods. "Sophie. My name is Sophie." Then something happens that Maxine would never have anticipated. Sophie reaches out and pulls Maxine to her, hugging her with a strength Maxine is amazed she possesses. After a brief moment, Sophie pulls away and grasps both of Maxine's hands in her own.

"Thank you," she says. "I'm sorry for you, too." Then she releases Maxine's hands and says, "You should go now. I need to see to Chloe." With that, Maxine is ushered out the door, which closes quietly behind her.

She's down the steps and across the street and sitting in her car with her keys in her lap before she grasps what just happened, whether it was good or bad.

CHAPTER ELEVEN

Michael sips coffee at the kitchen bar, waiting for Maxine to get up. They have unfinished business this morning, and he wants to get it over with so that he can enjoy his day without anything weighing on his mind. He's not proud of his behavior last night, but he also wants to know what's going on with her.

Maxine came home after an improbably long dinner with her priest friend, whom Michael has never met, and went straight to bed, claiming exhaustion. Michael sat up, struggling with conflicting emotions including anger, sympathy, frustration, guilt and, most inconvenient, desire. After a few glasses of wine, he joined Maxine upstairs. Climbing into bed naked and holding her from behind seemed appropriate at the time, but she groggily brushed him off like an annoying bug. He was humiliated, and his anger was immediate and intense.

"What the hell is that? Am I bothering you?" he demanded, sitting up and staring down at her. She didn't even turn her head, just laid with her back to him.

"Michael, please. I'm tired."

Had she at least turned to face him, maybe given him a kiss goodnight, he might have let it go, but this complete lack of courtesy was more than he could tolerate in his current state of mind. He grabbed her shoulder and turned her onto her back, more roughly than he intended. She pushed his hand off her and propped herself on her elbows.

"Jesus, Michael, what is the matter with you?"

"I haven't seen you in almost a week and you can't even turn around and look at me? All this shit that's going on, I'd think you could at least manage a quick fuck."

"You're drunk. Go to sleep, Michael." Maxine started to roll back onto her side, but Michael wasn't finished. He pushed her onto her back and straddled her hips so she'd have to face him. He felt like he deserved some answers. He just wasn't sure what the questions were. It didn't matter.

Maxine's palm met his nose in an upward direction with just enough force that he tasted blood immediately. She was out from under him and off the bed so quickly, she didn't even end up with blood on her. Through his pain, Michael watched her shake her head in disgust.

"That was nothing, by the way. I'm going to sleep now, because like I said, I'm fucking tired." With that, she left the room and he heard a door slam down the hall. After he cleaned up the blood and determined his nose wasn't broken, he went after her to apologize, but the door to the guest bedroom was locked.

In the light of day, Michael knows the first words out of his mouth must be, "I'm sorry." He's come to the disturbing realization that something in Maxine's past causes her to react with violence rather than fear when threatened. He wants to help her through this ordeal, regardless of what else is going on in his life, but he sees how he's been judging her instead. From a clinical perspective, he knows this is an easy trap to fall into, but counterproductive. He vows to suspend his judgment and stand by her as best he can. He plans to break off their engagement, but offer his support until this assault case is resolved. Remembering her birthday, he wonders how they got to this point so quickly, how he can be so ready to let her go. He can come to only one conclusion: Maxine left during a period of conflict, and the separation drove a wedge between them that their relationship couldn't withstand.

Maxine pads into the kitchen at around nine thirty in her pajamas. She pours a cup of coffee and stands across the bar from Michael. She looks rested and cheerful, not exactly what he was expecting.

"Maxine, I'm so sorry. I don't know what I was thinking."

Maxine nods. "Me too. I shouldn't have hit you."

"You know I would never hurt you, right?"

Maxine nods again. "It's not broken, is it?"

Michael touches his nose and winces, but shakes his head. "I know I haven't been very supportive the last couple of weeks, but I can't figure out what's going on with you. I don't know how to be with you right now, what you need from me." He thinks this sounds sincere and constructive, a good beginning.

Maxine blows on her coffee and takes a tentative sip. He wonders why she's stalling, and senses things are about to take an unexpected turn. For one thing, she doesn't seem angry. The argument for which he was preparing isn't materializing.

Maxine meets his gaze and Michael sees that something deep inside her has shifted. She says evenly, "You don't know what I need from you, but that's not all your fault. I could have done a better job of telling you. I shouldn't have made you guess."

Michael has the impression she's not talking about just the last couple of weeks. This puts him on the defensive, because he assumed she was happy in their relationship.

"And you don't know how to be with me because you don't really want to. If you did, this wouldn't be so hard. Or, it might be hard, but not impossible."

"What are you talking about?" Michael asks, flustered.

Maxine laughs, which Michael knows is her defense mechanism but still finds annoying.

"I'm trying to say you can do better than me. You can find someone you have more in common with, who doesn't have to work so hard to make you happy. I'm so tired of trying to be someone you can love unconditionally. It's exhausting, Michael."

Michael realizes that he couldn't have asked for an easier out. His ego, however, is having difficulty coping with being rejected, particularly since he has been agonizing over how not to hurt Maxine. He feigns relief he doesn't yet feel, but knows he will once he's had time.

"I'm so glad you feel that way. I mean, I'm here for you during this whole assault business, but I think we've both known for a while that the marriage wasn't going to happen."

Maxine looks surprised. "No, actually, I haven't. Why didn't you say something?"

Michael doesn't have a good answer for this, but he's happy to have saved face. "I don't know exactly. But there's no real point in digging through the ruins, is there?"

Maxine studies Michael, and he can almost feel her poking around in his brain. She shrugs with indifference, which is, of course, the ultimate affront. "No, I don't suppose there is."

Anthony is having another go at the wisteria arbor, this time with Sophie sitting on the back steps sipping coffee and helping him decide what to cut and where to direct the keepers. She seems distracted, and he wonders if something's up with Chloe. Not only did he skip the farmers market; it was also the first Saturday afternoon he missed with Chloe in years.

He succeeded in removing the robins' nest mostly intact, but Chloe and Sophie gave it only a cursory inspection when they got home. After breakfast and the requisite time spent reading the paper and digesting, Anthony cut the grass and bagged the clippings, tidied up the garden shed, then decided he had done enough for one day. His face was throbbing, and he headed into the kitchen, swallowed a couple of Vicodin and let Sophie know he was going to shower and take a nap. By the time he woke up, the house was dark and Sophie was asleep next to him.

Now he's eager to finish this project. "What do you think? Are we done?" It's warm this morning and Anthony is dripping sweat. Sophie glances up and scans the arbor, then nods. As Anthony descends the ladder, she gets up and walks over to him.

"Anthony." She glances over her shoulder toward the house as Anthony wipes sweat from his face and removes his gloves.

"What's the matter?" he asks, worried now.

Sophie keeps her voice low, presumably so Chloe won't hear. "Last night that woman came here." Seeing Anthony's blank look, she explains impatiently, "The woman who saw Chloe with Deon and took her from him."

"What did she want? Why didn't you tell me?"

"I'm telling you now, so hush. She came to say she was sorry, to say she made a mistake and she was sorry."

Anthony shakes his head in disbelief. "Her timing's pretty shitty. After everything Chloe's been through, now she decides she made a mistake — "

"That's not the point. Listen to me." It's Anthony's turn to be impatient as Sophie continues, "It wasn't her. It was Chloe. Chloe was in the kitchen and when she saw this woman at the door, she yelled her name and ran to her. Anthony, Chloe was happy to see her. Not scared. Happy."

It doesn't take Anthony long to see where Sophie is going with this. If some strange woman barged in and drop kicked Deon, then dragged Chloe to her house and called the police, why would Chloe be happy to see her?

"Did you talk to Chloe?" Anthony asks.

Sophie shakes her head. "This woman, Maxine. She's been arrested you know. She was so upset, but for us, and for Chloe, not for herself. And I don't think she was mistaken at all."

Anthony hurries into the kitchen, Sophie on his heels, and finds the big detective's card. He answers, "Detective Hancock" on the first ring and Anthony wonders if he's ever not working.

"It's Anthony Scialfa. I think Chloe's ready to talk."

"Do you think or do you know? It'll be tricky to get Dr. Webster to come in on a Sunday unless — "

"All due respect, Detective, try to imagine how little I care what day of the week it is." Sophie glances up, surprised. There's a long pause at the other end of the line.

"Fair enough. I'll call you back." Anthony nods to Sophie and takes the phone with him upstairs, where he jumps in the shower for a quick rinse while Sophie waits on the toilet seat with the phone in her hand. Anthony dries off and dresses, and he's putting on his shoes when the phone rings. They both jump. Sophie hands the phone to Anthony.

"Hello?"

"Can you be here in twenty minutes?"

"No problem." Anthony hangs up and looks at Sophie. "You have to stay here. Chloe will know something's up if you go." This is flimsy, but it's the best Anthony can come up with, and Sophie doesn't put up a fight this time. She just nods and hurries to get Chloe.

On the drive to the station, Chloe is understandably upset about this sudden development. Anthony tries to explain that Dr. Webster had a cancellation and wanted to squeeze

Chloe in since it has been almost a week since they last talked. When she starts to whine about it being a weekend, Anthony quiets her with a look, and they ride in silence.

Anthony parks the car and turns to Chloe. "This is it, Chloe. You have to talk to Dr. Webster and tell her the truth, no matter what. Do you understand me?"

Chloe doesn't respond, doesn't even look at him. Instead, she opens her car door and climbs out, leaving Anthony to follow her into the station.

"What makes you think she's ready?" Dr. Webster asks. Chloe sits on the floor of the interview room with Detectives Hancock and Laird. Dr. Webster wanted to talk to Anthony before she sees Chloe, and they watch her through the one-way glass.

"The woman who took her and called the police, what's her name?" Anthony asks.

"I have no idea. Why?"

"She came to our house last night, to apologize. When Chloe saw her, she called her name and ran to her. She was happy to see her. Why do you suppose that is?"

Dr. Webster appears disappointed that this is Anthony's big news. "It could mean something, or it could just be that Chloe thinks she's interesting. It's a new angle I can use, though. Can't hurt." With that, she's out the door. When she appears in the other room, the two detectives leave and join Anthony. Dr. Webster sits on the floor with Chloe. Detective Laird flips a switch so they can listen.

"Last time we talked you told me a little about your mom and dad and your Uncle Deon. You seemed pretty worried about your mom. How is she doing?"

Chloe stares at her shoes and says, "She's good. She's better. We went shopping for my dad's birthday, just the two of us. And we went to the market alone together yesterday."

"I'm happy to hear that, Chloe. That must be a big relief for you, huh?"

Chloe nods.

"Your dad tells me you saw someone last night that you hadn't seen in a while. What's her name again?"

Chloe brightens. "Maxine."

"That's right, Maxine. How did you feel about seeing her?"

Chloe shrugs, suddenly guarded, and says, "Okay."

"Can you tell me a little bit about Maxine? How old is she? What's she like?"

"She's older, like my mom. She's cool, I guess. She's got long blond hair and these neat old boots. And a suede jacket."

Dr. Webster nods as if this is exactly what she wanted to know, then furrows her brow and asks, "She was wearing that last night? It was a little warm for boots and a jacket, wasn't it?"

Chloe shakes her head. "No, she was wearing it the day she brought me to her house."

"Oh, right. Did you know her before then?"

"No."

"But you went to her house with her. Weren't you afraid?"

"No." Chloe is beginning to look nervous. Anthony starts to pace like a caged animal.

"Your mom and dad must have taught you not to get into cars with strangers — "

"We walked," Chloe corrects Dr. Webster.

"Oh. Okay, you walked. But still, you went home with a total stranger and you weren't scared?"

Chloe jumps up then and walks to the mirror. She pretends to smooth her hair, but Anthony sees the panic in her eyes. He stops pacing right in front of her and stares at his terrified little girl, feeling his own fear building.

Dr. Webster also stands. "Chloe? Can you tell me why you went home with Maxine that day?"

Anthony sees the moment Chloe snaps. Her fear turns to panic and she spins around to face Dr. Webster.

"I know what you're trying to do and it won't work!" she screams, her voice shrill and quivering. She stands with her hands clenched in fists at her sides. "Stop it, just stop it!"

Dr. Webster continues calmly, "I'm just curious, Chloe. What was it that made you go with Maxine that day even though — "

Chloe charges at Dr. Webster, her little fists pummeling her torso. "You can't make me tell! You can't do it!"

Dr. Webster drops to her knees and wraps her arms around Chloe, containing her violent outburst and holding her tight while she struggles. Chloe starts to cry furiously.

"What will happen if you tell? What will happen, Chloe?" she asks above Chloe's sobs. "Tell me what will happen."

"She'll die! Mommy will die and it'll be my fault! I'm not going to tell you! I'm not!" Chloe's protests are weaker now, and she's less angry than hysterical. As Dr. Webster continues to hold her, Chloe's arms go limp and drop to her sides, her little body racked with sobs.

Anthony paces helplessly. He doesn't think he can take much more of this. "Stop this. It's too much for her."

The detectives watch this scene, rapt. Detective Laird, says, "No, this is good. She's close now. This is it."

Dr. Webster strokes Chloe's hair and murmurs, "Who told you that? Who told you Mommy would die?"

"He did! Deon said if I told anyone it would upset Mommy so much that she wouldn't get better!"

Anthony springs for the door, but Detective Hancock catches him and holds him in a bear hug from behind, restraining him as easily as he lifted Chloe the other day to get a soda.

Detective Laird looks at Anthony and says, "We don't have him yet. And even when we do, it won't do Chloe any good to see you like this. You'll need to talk to Dr. Webster and calm down first. Understood?" Anthony nods, fuming.

Dr. Webster continues holding Chloe, whispering, "Okay, okay. It's okay, Chloe," until Chloe's crying subsides enough for her to talk. Then Dr. Webster pulls away and holds Chloe by the shoulders, ducking her head until Chloe meets her gaze.

"That's not true, you know. Your mom's getting better every day, you said so yourself. And even if she wasn't, it wouldn't have anything to do with you telling."

Chloe's wet, splotchy face is skeptical. She croaks, "I just want Mommy to be okay. I'll do anything."

Dr. Webster nods. "I know you would. But what

Uncle Deon told you isn't true. Your mom's a smart lady, isn't she?"

Chloe nods vigorously, hiccupping from crying.

"Well, then she probably already knows more than you think. I'll bet she wishes she knew everything. Sometimes it's harder to know a little bit of something upsetting than to know all of it. Does that make sense?"

Chloe nods again, but with less conviction.

"Yeah, that's a little confusing. How about this: do you think maybe you could trust me with your secret? Then we can decide if your mom would feel better knowing everything, if it might help her stop worrying."

There is a long silence. Finally, almost imperceptibly, Chloe's head bobs up and down. She leans over and whispers into Dr. Webster's ear. Dr. Webster's face registers no reaction. When Chloe finishes and pulls away, Dr. Webster smiles at her and gives her a big hug.

"You're a brave girl, Chloe. But I need you to be a little braver. You see, when you whisper a secret, it's still just a secret. Do you think you can say it out loud? Say exactly what you just said to me, only out loud this time."

Chloe voice is barely audible. "Deon would put his hand on me and then touch his privates. He'd, you know, rub his penis."

"Would he rub it inside his pants or outside?"

"Inside."

"Where did he put his hand on you?"

Chloe hesitates. "Usually just on my leg." She points to her upper thigh.

"Anywhere else that you remember?"

Chloe fidgets, then points between her legs.

"Remember to say it out loud, Chloe."

"Between my legs."

"Okay. Inside your pants or outside?"

"Outside."

"Okay. Is there anything else you can think of? Anything at all, no matter how small it seems."

Chloe shakes her head, and then says firmly, "No."

"How many times do you think this happened? You don't have to be exact, just guess."

"Just a few times. Maybe three or four."

"Okay. You did great, Chloe. And you know what? We're done for now. I'm going to talk to your father for a minute, and in a little while you can see your mom. And I promise you she'll look just as well as when you left her." Dr. Webster smiles and squeezes Chloe's hand, with a glance at the mirror.

Detective Laird hurries out of the room. Detective Hancock loosens his grip on Anthony just enough to turn off the sound to the interview room and close the blinds. When Dr. Webster enters, he releases Anthony and positions himself by the door.

Dr. Webster motions for Anthony to sit at the table, then sits across from him. "I'm sorry, Mr. Scialfa. That must have been difficult to see. Not exactly the outcome we were looking for." She pauses. "Right now I need to make sure you're okay before you see Chloe. How you behave with her right now is critical. Your wife should hear this, too. Can she join us?"

Anthony nods and says, "I'll call her. But I think I'm okay." Oddly, Anthony is okay. He's so sad for Chloe his chest aches, and he wants to wrap her in his arms and keep her safe forever, but he's always felt that way about her; the intensity has simply ratcheted up several notches.

He dreads telling Sophie, but he takes out his cell phone and calls home. When she answers, he says, "Can you meet us here?" She agrees and he can tell by the sound of her voice that she already knows. He hangs up and meets Dr. Webster's gaze. "I hope you're right. That it's better she know."

Dr. Webster briefs Anthony on how best to interact with Chloe, but he realizes she's not telling him anything he doesn't already know. Of course he won't become hysterical, or distant. He won't press her to talk about what she's been through, or treat her any differently than usual. He'll tell her she's a brave little girl, and he loves her and always will. No big surprises there.

Dr. Webster adds, "You may not want to let on that you just saw the whole thing. You could tell her I said she did great, something to that effect. Chloe should continue therapy to help her process what's happened to her, to make sure she knows it's not her fault. She can remain with me if she's comfortable, but she may feel as though I've betrayed her confidence and prefer to talk to someone else. If that's the case, I can refer you to someone excellent." Dr. Webster pauses. "Okay, that's it. Why don't you go sit with her while we wait for your wife?"

"Thank you. You're very good at what you do, aren't you?" Dr. Webster smiles. As Anthony gets up to leave, he pauses and turns to Dr. Webster. "My wife, Sophie, may be a little more difficult. Don't take it personally."

Dr. Webster replies, "I never do."

Detective Hancock opens the door and says, "Suspect will most likely be in custody by the end of the day. If he makes bail, steer clear." He gestures toward Anthony's battered face. "Probably should've told you that last week." Anthony nods curtly and goes to hug Chloe.

Chloe feels like she's on a rollercoaster, but blindfolded so she can't see where it's going next. This morning with Dr. Webster was a major drag, and she's sure she would have done better with some warning. But when it's over and she's home with her mom and dad, it's almost as if nothing happened. Both of them tell her how much they love her, which they do all the time anyway, and then her dad asks her what she wants to do with their afternoon together, since he slept through yesterday.

They go to the pool, and Chloe plays with her friends while her father watches every second to make sure she doesn't drown. Sometimes his worrying so much bothers her, but today all she can think about is whether or not her mom is at home dying. They don't stay as long as usual, and on the way home he doesn't ask her if she has any questions about her mom. He just says, "Your mom's getting better every day, you know that, right?" She nods and wishes he'd drive faster so they can get home and make sure her mom is still alive.

When they pull into the garage, Chloe is out the door the second the car stops. She finds her mom in the living room, curled up on the couch writing a letter on thin paper. Chloe can tell she's been crying. Her heart drops and she flings herself onto the floor at her feet.

"What's wrong, Mommy?"

"Nothing, mon petit chou, I was just writing a letter to an old friend. How was the pool?" She folds the paper carefully and sets it aside, then pats the sofa next to her. Chloe climbs up and snuggles into her mother's side, the good side that isn't still sore sometimes. Her mom wraps one arm around her and holds her tight, and strokes her damp hair with the other hand.

"Chloe, I want to tell you something, and it's important, très important, that you listen to me. Okay?"

Chloe is certain this is it. Her mom is going to tell her that her other breast is sick and that this time they can't fix it. She nods a tiny bit, her dark lashes already wet.

"I'm going to be fine. My sickness, they caught it so early, and my treatment went very well. But I need you to do something for me that will be a big help. I need you to stop all of this worrying about me. It reminds me that I was sick and I don't want to think about it all the time. Okay?"

The rollercoaster swerves sharply to the side just when Chloe thought it was about to drop. Chloe lifts her head and stares at her mom with her mouth hanging open.

"Can you do that for me?" her mom asks, brushing a clump of wet hair from Chloe's cheek. Chloe nods, tears spilling down her cheeks.

"Do you promise?" her mom asks, holding out her pinkie. They haven't made a pinkie swear in as long as Chloe can remember. Chloe wraps her little pinkie around her mom's and they both squeeze tight and giggle.

Without letting go, Chloe says quietly, "Do you promise you won't get sick again?"

Her mom sighs and her smile fades, but she holds

onto Chloe's finger. "I can't do that, Chloe. I'm okay now and I promise nothing you do will make me sick again. But you can help me by being strong and by being honest, and by not worrying so much. Do you believe me, Chloe?"

The rollercoaster slows to a crawl. Chloe needs to think really hard. She wanted to believe her mom when she told her it was nobody's fault that her grandpa died, or when people got sick. It was so tempting, but she needed to feel like she was helping, like she had some control. Now her mom is telling her that she wasn't helping in the first place, that her worrying makes it worse. And this morning Dr. Webster, a doctor, told her that Uncle Deon was lying. Can it be this simple?

"Chloe." Her mom puts a finger under Chloe's chin and tilts her head up. "Do you believe me?"

"Yes, Mommy," Chloe whispers. And she does.

Maxine is in the office upstairs, packing her books into boxes, when the phone rings. She hears Michael answer it in the bedroom, where he is spending a ridiculous amount of time trying to decide what to wear to some work party.

He appears in the doorway with the phone. "It's Tom. The lawyer." He says the word "lawyer" in a bored tone, as if the fact that she has a lawyer is just one more reason that they couldn't possibly be wed.

Maxine is sitting on the floor, and she holds out a hand so that he has to bring the phone to her. She hopes she hasn't done damage to her case by apologizing to the Scialfas, but she isn't sorry she did it. She's baffled by Sophie's reaction, but doesn't believe it was negative.

"Hello?" she says nervously.

"Max — can I call you Max? Doesn't really matter, I guess, since this is probably the last time we'll be talking. Let's hope so, anyway." He laughs at his joke, which Maxine doesn't get, then continues, "The charges against you have been dropped. Case dismissed without prejudice. Little girl gave it up this morning. Suspect is in custody and the ADA thinks you're more of a hero than a felon. So go on about you business. And don't have a coronary when you get my bill." He laughs again.

"I don't understand. What happened?" Maxine asks, not sure she understands what he's telling her.

"Like I said, the little girl finally talked to the cops, and you were right about the uncle. Hadn't been going on for very long, but once is enough, right? You're off the hook regardless of how the case against him turns out, since the victim corroborates your account of the incident."

Maxine's eyes fill with tears and she wishes Michael would stop staring at her. She turns away from his gaze, conflicting waves of relief and sadness crashing against her ribcage. She breathes deeply to steady her voice and asks, "Is she okay? Chloe, I mean. Will she have to testify?"

"I can't tell you for sure. Her interview was videotaped, so the prosecutor will most likely use that if the case goes to trial, which I doubt. My guess, he cuts a deal. Which is good news for you, since you won't have to testify, either. It's not fun." There's a pause, and when Tom continues his voice is subdued. "Look, I know you feel bad for her, that's perfectly natural. But try to focus on the fact that you did the right thing, and because of that she has a shot at a normal life."

Maxine laughs harshly, more of a bark, really. "Normal? You really believe that?"

"I don't know, kiddo, I don't know. Listen, take care of yourself, okay?" And then he's gone.

Maxine becomes aware of the fact that Michael is pacing frenetically behind her, which gives her some perverse comfort. She holds the phone and wonders whom to tell first. She dials, waits, and then says, "Luce? They got him. It's over." As Lucy squeals on her end, Maxine turns to smile at Michael, who is suddenly still. He walks over and puts a hand on Maxine's shoulder, then turns and leaves her to her conversation.

Once he's gone, Maxine tells Lucy she'll call her back. She dials Jay's number, from memory. She has thought constantly about calling him, but decided to wait until she had news. He must have caller ID, because he answers, "God, I miss you. What took you so long? What's going on?"

Maxine's exoneration is a huge relief to Michael. Mostly for her sake, of course, but it also makes their parting less complicated, and allows him to contemplate his future with less foreboding and more immediacy. Right now, his future is an afternoon at Michelle's home, and he must admit, the casual barbeque has him stumped as far as attire was concerned. He settles on a pair of jeans and a charcoal grey T-shirt, along with black sandals that Maxine assures him aren't too gay.

He parks across the street from Michelle's house, a boxy, contemporary, two-story affair he suspects is environmentally cutting-edge. Again, he's bemused that she lives in such a trendy neighborhood. He grabs a bottle of top-shelf pinot noir from the passenger seat before locking the car and setting the alarm. Then he strides up the driveway to the front entrance.

After a long wait that prompts him to double check the house number and ring the bell again, the front door opens and Michelle smiles. Music drifts from outside. "Michael, you made it! Come in, we're out back. Were you waiting? Sometimes I can't hear the bell." She takes Michael's arm and leads him to the back patio, through the center of the house. From what he glimpses, the interior of the house is chic and uncluttered, and he looks forward to exploring it further. The polished concrete floor flows seamlessly from inside to out, thanks to a garage style door of metal and glass that slides up and overhead.

A dozen or so guests mingle on the back patio, and Michael is struck by how the scene resembles a page out of a style magazine. He's relieved to be dressed appropriately, and very much aware of Michelle's hand on his arm.

Michelle calls, "Hey everybody, this is Michael." People turn and nod, smiling, and Michael smiles back. Michelle says more quietly to Michael, "Michael, this is everybody." She notices the bottle of wine he's holding. "Let's add that to the bar and get you a drink." She leads him to one end of the patio where a few guests linger around a long outdoor table that serves as a bar, replete with a large metal tub full of ice to chill the white wines and beer, an impressive selection of red wines and some hard liquor, including a few bottles of quality Scotch.

Soft Landing

Michael sets his wine next to the other unopened reds and tries to decide what he's in the mood for.

"Ooh, nice pinot!" Michael and Michelle turn toward the male voice so impressed with Michael's contribution to the bar. Its owner is tan and fit, a bit shorter than Michael, and in his mid to late thirties, Michael estimates. He holds out a hand and says, "Michael was it? I'm Peter."

They shake hands. "Nice to meet you, Peter," Michael replies. Thus begins a series of introductions and brief but pleasant conversations as Michael makes his way through the crowd in search of Michelle, who vanished once Michael had a drink in hand. He chose a Washington pinot gris, determined to broaden his horizons by seeking out quality local wines. Now he finishes his wine, which is surprisingly good, and swallows a pita wedge dipped in hummus. He spies Michelle by a giant gas grill, piling a platter with skewers of meats and vegetables. He sets his empty glass on a nearby table and makes his way over to her.

"Need a hand with that?" he inquires. He startles her, but she gratefully hands him the heavy platter.

"Thank God," she laughs, and continues taking kabobs from the grill and stacking them with both hands. Michael sees that she has barbequed a combination of beef and scallops, along with cherry tomatoes, yellow bell peppers and broccoli florets, a sort of surf and turf in a colorful and inventive presentation. Michael is quite impressed.

"I don't know where the hell Amy is," Michelle grumbles. "She always disappears when there's work to do." Michael has no idea who Amy is, but he is happy to help. He studies Michelle in her casual attire — a slim, brightly patterned knee length skirt with beads around the hem, and a gauzy T-shirt layered over a ribbed tank. She's barefoot, and he's pretty sure she's not wearing a bra. Tan and lean, she's even more appealing to him in this setting than in the office.

As Michelle sets the last skewer on the platter, a woman appears and asks brightly, "What can I do?" She has dark, close-cropped hair and wears a tight black T-shirt and jeans. She's attractive, Michael supposes, but in a boyish sort of way.

"Perfect timing," Michelle replies. "We're done." The woman puts an arm around Michelle's waist and looks at her with an exaggerated expression of remorse, pleading forgiveness. Michelle ignores this and says, "This is Michael, the therapist from work I told you about. Michael, this is Amy. My partner."

Amy extends a hand but slaps her forehead when she sees that both of Michael's hands are occupied. She grins. "It's nice to finally meet you, Michael. I've heard a lot about you."

Michael twists his lips into what he hopes resembles a smile and replies, "Nice to meet you, too." The platter of kabobs is warm and becoming increasingly heavy, and he feels a bead of sweat run down his forehead.

"God, I'm sorry, that must weigh a ton," Michelle exclaims. "You can put it in the middle of the table with the rest of the food. Thanks, Michael. You're a life saver."

Michael turns and makes his way to the food table, placing the heavy platter carefully in an empty space in the center. He wipes the sweat from his face and heads straight to the bar for a real drink.

Once the Scotch kicks in and Michael is pleasantly buzzed, he decides to make the most of the evening. He enjoys the food and participates in conversations, but he can't stop wondering how he could have so thoroughly misread Michelle's signals. As a psychologist, he'd like to believe he is above average at reading people. Granted, he works exclusively with children, and adults present an entirely different set of challenges, but did she or did she not flirt outrageously with him at the bar less than a week ago?

With an empty plate and a full bladder, Michael excuses himself from his current circle of dinner companions and makes his way into the house in search of a bathroom. He finds a powder room that is so spare and elegant he hates to spoil it with his presence, but he relieves himself and washes up, then stares at his reflection in the mirror as he dries his hands on a neatly pressed linen hand towel. He realizes this development is probably for the best, that it would have been a mistake to jump from one relationship to another. What he needs now is a simple transitional companion. And as long as he's here, why pass up any opportunity this evening might present to get laid?

Michael steps back outside, helps himself to another Scotch at the bar and turns to take stock of the crowd. He sees a few attractive women, but they seem to be partnered with men or, in a few cases, other women. Not surprising, he surmises, given the party's hostesses. Most of the other guests are men, many with whom he has already spoken, or who appear to be couples.

Michael feels an arm brush up against his and turns to find Michelle at his side. He is still aroused by her proximity, and this irritates him, but he raises his glass and says wryly, "To unwinding."

Michelle grins and raises her own glass, then leans in and asks, "Anyone in particular you'd like to unwind with? Peter's kind of exuberant, like a puppy that wants to lick you all over, but that might not be so bad."

The last piece of the puzzle floats into place in Michael's alcohol marinated brain. It's so perfect he wonders how it took him so long to catch on. Dr. Besser believes that he is gay.

CHAPTER TWELVE

Maxine awakens early in the guest bedroom, eager to greet the day for the first time in as long as she can remember. *Moving day.* She realized yesterday there was nothing keeping her here, and suddenly she couldn't wait to get home. She rolls over and savors the word: *home.* She hasn't really thought of Bozeman as home for a long time, but everything is there for her now, and the ghosts of her past no longer seem as real a threat. She will see Astrid's daughter grow. She will finally get to know her sister, particularly since Lucy has agreed to let her live with her until she finds her own place. She will make every effort to have at least a cordial relationship with her mother, and hope for more.

And there's Jay. Thinking about him makes her giddy, but she wants to take things slowly. She wants to be deliberate in making decisions about their relationship, to make sure she takes care of herself as much as she wants to take care of him. They are both a little banged up emotionally, and she reminds herself that one night of physical and emotional coupling, no matter how intense, doesn't guarantee anything. Then she laughs into her pillow, because she knows she will fling herself with abandon into this unknown territory, that if he wants her, he can have every last bit of her. She knows this because she is consumed with wanting every cell of him. She's nervous about the intensity of her feelings, and the unknowable future that awaits her, but trying not to love him now would be like jumping off a bridge and trying to stop herself mid-fall.

She wishes she had told Michael she would be leaving today before he left for his party, but she hadn't known. Everything happened so quickly. She called Father Brian to bring him up to date and to thank him for his friendship and guidance. On a whim, Maxine invited him to drive home with her. He had a small break in his schedule that would require they leave right away, and she couldn't think of a single reason not to.

While on the phone with Brian, she walked from room to room in the house, Michael's house, and realized that all she needed to bring were her books, clothes and personal belongings. Every stitch of furniture she ever owned was eliminated over the years as she deferred to Michael's design expertise. When Brian asked if she could rent a truck so last minute, she realized she didn't need one and laughed.

"You know, I think my Blazer will do the trick." She may have emotional baggage, but her worldly possessions certainly weren't weighing her down. "I have a lot of books, mostly."

"Oh, fantastic. Just books. Any chance your ex will help you pack up?" Brian asked hopefully.

Soft Landing

Maxine assured Brian she was capable of carrying book boxes to her car, a decision she regretted soon after she started, and again as she sits up in bed and feels throbbing pain in her arms and back.

Her clothes she laid in the back of the car, and the rest, mostly memorabilia, framed photos, her laptop and some miscellaneous items, went into suitcases or boxes.

She didn't feel right taking the jewelry that Michael had given her, but leaving anything other than the engagement ring seemed ungrateful. She didn't want to belabor the fact that it wasn't her taste, but she knew she would never wear it. She decided to talk to him about it when he got home, and packed up everything else.

By the time Maxine decided to quit for the night, Michael still wasn't home. She hoped he wasn't avoiding her because of last night's debacle. She waited up for a while, but wanted to get a good night's sleep for the drive tomorrow. She went to bed early and slept like a baby for the first time in weeks.

Her watch tells her it's six thirty, so Maxine gets out of bed painfully and hurries to catch Michael before he leaves for work. She finds him in the kitchen slumped over the counter, waiting for the coffee to finish brewing. He hasn't showered, and he is pale and puffy. When he pours a cup of coffee, his hands shake.

"Yikes. Some party, huh?" she asks.

Michael mutters, "Oh, it was some party all right."

Michael would prefer time to think things through before he and Maxine have another go around, but for some reason she's determined to talk now. He's running late, and is distracted by a bad night's sleep, a hangover, and the fact that he will be seeing Sean again today. Suddenly Maxine is saying something about moving out.

"What are you talking about?" he snaps. He doesn't want to seem like a prick, so he softens his tone and asks, "I'm sorry, baby. I've got kind of a long day ahead of me. What were you saying?"

"I wanted to tell you last night, but you came home after I went to bed." Maxine is wearing a tank and boxers and her hair is tousled from sleep, and he wishes she didn't look so sexy.

"Are you still mad about the other night? Because you can take your time if you're really leaving. You don't have to worry about me pouncing on you again." He says this last part teasingly.

"Um, I don't get it. I thought you'd be happy to have me out of your hair." Maxine is flustered and looks to Michael for guidance. He misses that, knowing that she'll turn to him in times of uncertainty. He thought he'd always be that person.

Michael walks around the breakfast bar to where Maxine stands. He brushes a strand of hair from her forehead. "How the hell did we end up here? It just feels like everything fell apart so fast, doesn't it?"

Maxine nods tentatively and shifts from one foot to the other. "I guess so. I'm sorry, Michael, I really am."

"I know. I'm sorry, too." Michael pulls Maxine into a hug. She stiffens at first, then relaxes and returns the hug, though less enthusiastically than Michael would like. Aware of her braless breasts against his chest, he pulls her closer and whispers, "God, I miss you."

In an instant, Maxine wrenches free and backs up, gaping at him. "What are you doing?" she demands.

Michael is suddenly angry, too, but does his best to hide it so she doesn't hit him again. He's so tired of trying to guess what these fucking women want. He keeps his voice calm as he says, "I'm just trying to figure out what's going on here, Max. Is this it, really? Three years and you're ready to move out just like that? I ask you to take your time and you behave as if you're all packed and can't get out of here fast enough."

"I am packed. That's what I was trying to tell you. I'm leaving this morning." She looks pained, and Michael realizes what an idiot he must seem to her. He feels his face burn with confusion and embarrassment.

"This morning." Michael glances around, seeing nothing missing. His head throbs. "What do you mean, you're packed? Where exactly are you planning to go?"

"I'm driving to Bozeman. Father Brian's going with me, and he had to leave today so he could get back for — " She trails off and waves a hand dismissively. "Whatever. I'm packed and I'm leaving today."

On his way to work, Michael wishes Maxine hadn't forced their last moments together to be rushed and unpleasant, that she had shown some respect for the three years they had shared together. Instead, she caught him off guard, and he made a fool of himself. He was feeling acutely alone after last night, and she looked so vulnerable standing there in her pajamas.

He is still smarting from the discussion of the jewelry. Did she need to remind him how much money he had spent on her? He supposes she was aiming for diplomacy when she claimed she loved it all, but wouldn't feel right taking it without talking to him first. He suspects the real truth is that she never fully appreciated the subtle taste and beauty of each piece, that she could take it or leave it. He had no qualms accepting the engagement ring, since they were no longer engaged, and it had cost a fortune. Ultimately, Maxine yielded and packed the rest. Since Michael had insisted, however, he doesn't even have the luxury of resenting her greed.

When Michael stepped into their closet to dress and was confronted with the emptiness of Maxine's half, he realized that he would have to sell the house. He makes good money and expects his client list to grow, but their neighborhood is expensive, and Maxine's income helped cover the mortgage. This is perhaps the most infuriating repercussion of her leaving. She took almost nothing with her and didn't even mention her portion of the down payment, yet Michael will still be forced to find a cheaper house in an inferior neighborhood.

As he gets off the elevator and enters the main lobby of his offices, Michael tries to shed the feelings of abandonment and regret this morning foisted upon him. He needs his head in the right place for his third session with Sean, who is his first patient today. He was lucky to catch Sean's mother at home to let her know he was running late and needed to push back their appointment. This was possible because his next client wasn't scheduled until ten o'clock, although he hopes to have fewer gaps in his schedule as his practice grows.

He's relieved to not find them waiting in the lobby, and hurries to his office to gather his thoughts and review the notes he made over the weekend after reading the articles Dr. Besser left him, along with her recommendations. Sean's is the most compelling case he's had in his career, and he wants to be sure the boy receives the best possible treatment.

A little after nine, Sean's arrival is signaled by a buzzer and a light on the wall next to Michael's desk. He's ready, and he goes to escort them back to his office.

In the lobby, Michael says, "Hi there, Sean," to the little boy, and then smiles warmly at his mother. "You'll join us for a few minutes today?" he queries.

She nods, then asks in a nervous voice, "Actually, can I talk to you alone first?"

"Uh, of course. Will Sean be okay here?"

Sean's mom squats next to him and quietly asks him to sit in a chair and wait for her. She hands him a children's book from her purse, then follows Michael down the hallway to his office. He closes the door and sits in his large chair in the center of the room, rather than at his desk, and waits as Sean's mother settles on the couch in front of him.

"You'd prefer to talk about Sean's treatment plan without him present?" Michael inquires rhetorically, just to get the ball rolling.

She nods. After some hesitation, she says, "His father and I were thinking about that woman psychiatrist you mentioned, the one you wanted to consult with about Sean."

Michael nods. "Dr. Besser. Of course. I hope that isn't a problem. She's been able to give me some good input and steer me toward some research that I think might be very beneficial for Sean's case. That's why I wanted to include you today, to talk about the possibility of introducing medication as part of Sean's treatment."

"That's sort of what my husband and I figured, and we were wondering if it might make more sense for Sean to start seeing her instead. I mean, since she's the one who would prescribe the medication."

"I see. You know, it's very common to not see any progress after only two sessions. In fact, Dr. Besser has proposed a timetable of six to twelve weeks."

"Oh no, that's not it. I mean, it's not that we don't think you're doing a good job. It's just that it seems like it would be easier if Sean was talking directly to the person who was in charge of his medication."

"Of course, of course. I understand if you'd prefer Sean see a psychiatrist, and Dr. Besser is extremely competent."

"We were also thinking — and tell me if this is silly — we wonder if Sean might be more comfortable talking to a woman. You know, since the attacker was a man."

"I don't think that's silly at all. Whatever you and your husband think will work best for Sean." Michael smiles.

"I'm so sorry if we wasted your time."

"Don't give it another thought. What is best for the patient is always of paramount importance. This kind of referral happens all the time." Michael tries to recall ever losing a patient this way before, and cannot.

Soft Landing

Michael provides Sean's mother with Dr. Besser's business card. They agree there is no point in going ahead with today's visit, and once she is gone, Michael organizes Sean's file. He emails Dr. Besser, apprising her of his decision to refer Sean's case to her, given her considerable experience and clear desire to be involved with Sean's treatment. He assures her Sean's parents are in agreement, so she should expect a call soon.

With forty-five minutes to kill before his next client, Michael kicks back at his desk and takes stock. He realizes all he has lost, and a single thought occurs to him. *None of this would be happening if I hadn't taken Maxine to that ridiculous children's parade.*

Chloe sleeps so late that her mom finally comes into her bedroom to check on her. She climbs into bed and whispers in Chloe's ear, "Wake up, my little sleepy head." They snuggle, her mom tickling Chloe's bare arm so she gets goose bumps.

"I have something to show you," her mom says, sitting up. Chloe rolls onto her back. Her mom pulls off the scarf covering her head, and Chloe gasps. Her mother's head is covered with fine, dark brown fuzz. No more clumps and bald spots. Her mom has kept her scarf on all the time lately, so Chloe didn't know what was under there, but guessed her mom was wearing it because her hair was getting worse and she didn't want them to see it.

"I shaved the clumps last week when I saw new hair growing back, so it would be all one length, and voilà! I think it's très chic, non?" Her eyes twinkle.

"It's beautiful, Mommy," Chloe whispers. Her mom ducks her head so that Chloe can run a hand over the soft new hair. It tickles her palm and Chloe giggles.

"By the time we go on holiday, maybe it will look like I wanted it so short." Her mom looks as if she's doing math in her head. Chloe's heart flip flops in her chest.

"We're going this year? Really? When? Where?" Chloe blurts excitedly, sitting up and bouncing on the bed.

"Of course we're going, ma fille, at the end of the month when your father finishes his project. And this year we're going to Rouen. I miss my family, and I want them to see that I'm well, so they might stop worrying."

Chloe jumps out of bed and dances around her room, singing, "We're going to France! We're going to France!" Her mom watches her and laughs.

Chloe and her mom are at the kitchen island, eating a lunch of chicken salad and berries from the farmers market. Chloe is working up the nerve to ask her mom something that she's been wondering about all morning. She's half listening to her mom list everything that must be done before they leave.

"Um, Mom?" Chloe interrupts. When her mom looks up, Chloe can feel her face getting red, but she starts talking before she loses her nerve. "Since Gampa, you know, isn't here anymore, and your whole family is in France, do you want us to live there now instead of here?"

Her mom's brow furrows. "No, I never really thought about it that way. Why? Do you want to? Do you not like it here anymore, Chloe?"

"I like it okay. But France is so cool, and I thought you might be tired of being so far away from home."

"Well, I miss my family, of course, and my friends. But this is my home. I love being here with you and your father. I can't imagine even leaving this house, much less moving halfway around the world."

"So you're not sorry Daddy made you live here?"

"Oh, Chloe, Daddy didn't make me live here! He was ready to live in France if that's what I wanted. But we talked about it and it just made more sense to stay here."

"Why?"

"I'm not sure. I guess because we were happy here. I love France, and I do miss it, but now my home is here. You didn't think I was unhappy here, did you?"

When Chloe doesn't say anything, her mom gets up and lifts her off her barstool, holding her like she did when she was little, like her father still does, Chloe's arms around her neck and her legs wrapped around her waist. She squeezes her and rocks back and forth. Chloe can't believe her mom is strong enough to carry her like this, so she holds on tight.

"You're so much like your father. You worry too much, poor thing. Pauvre Chloe, what can I do to make you stop worrying?"

Her mom sets her down and squats in front of her. "I love it here, but tell me the truth — do you love it, too?"

Chloe thinks about it really hard and decides that she does love it here. She nods, and right now, she isn't worried about anything at all.

Anthony's postponed meeting with the Seattle couple goes smoothly, and he feels a little guilty for resenting them, even if he was wallowing in grief and self-pity at the time. The truth is, Anthony wouldn't have a job if it weren't for people like them, because building green, while commendable, is also quite expensive. He loves his job and the opportunity it gives him to make a difference, or at least to try.

So today, he does his best to leave his worries behind him, and throws himself back into his work with renewed focus and enthusiasm. A few colleagues remark on his bruised face, and he responds with a variety of stupid jokes about Sophie's French temper, how he'd been meaning to fix that loose step before someone fell on their face, how he doesn't understand why people say "It's just like riding a bike," when riding a bike is really dangerous. The only joke to which he does not resort is, "You should see the other guy." To the best of his knowledge, the other guy is languishing in jail without the luxury of bail, and he'd rather not start thinking about why.

On his way home from work, Anthony experiences what he is able to perceive only as a physical sensation. To be precise, he feels the absence of several physical sensations that have become constant. The back of his neck is not stretched taut like a rubber band about to snap. The pit of his stomach is just the pit of his stomach, rather than home to a family of knots, each representing a specific source of stress. His breathing is not shallow and his jaw is not clenched. He feels lighter, too, so much so that he wonders if he's lightheaded and actually having some sort of stroke. Then he laughs at his own paranoia and calls

Soft Landing

Sophie on his cell phone to suggest he pick up something to grill tonight.

Since it's such a beautiful night, they decide to eat dinner outside, and the grilled salmon, sweet corn on the cob and tangy potato salad taste even better accompanied by the smell of jasmine wafting from a neighbor's yard. Chloe and Sophie have been talking almost nonstop about their trip, and Anthony hopes that Sophie wasn't premature in telling her. So many things could interfere with their plans: his project could run past schedule; Deon's trial, if there is one, could start earlier than expected; Chloe may have to testify if her recorded testimony is ruled inadmissible; Chloe's therapist might think the trip is a bad idea.

Sophie catches him watching and smiles. She reaches a hand across the table and squeezes one of his. He knows she sees the concern on his face, and it affects her. He remembers the unusual feeling he had earlier in the car, and he wonders if that sort of relaxation is what normal people feel all the time, if that's how strong men feel. He wonders if he can choose to stop being so anxious. He thinks not. But as he watches his two beautiful girls planning excitedly what to pack, where to eat, where to shop and what sights to revisit, he decides to stop worrying right now and appreciate that his family is happy and safe tonight. And for tonight, it's enough.

After ten hours of driving, Maxine and Brian have run out of things to talk about and are getting on each other's nerves. Their relief is palpable as they enter the Bozeman city limits, and after a brief drive through town, Maxine pulls to a stop in front of Turn the Page. Lucy told Maxine to call an hour before their arrival so she could make sure they found parking. Maxine laughs when she sees Lucy has accomplished this by placing a few bright orange construction cones in the parking space directly in front of the bookstore.

"What in the world?" Brian asks.

"It's just Lucy, you know, exercising her 28th amendment right to do whatever the hell she wants," Maxine replies with amusement and admiration. "Go move 'em, will you?"

Brian turns to regard Maxine with obvious displeasure at being bossed around.

"Fine, I'll do it," she says, but the point becomes moot as Lucy trots out of the store and moves the cones. Maxine waves, then pulls ahead and backs into the space.

Maxine steps out of the Blazer, her tailbone screaming in agony. She waddles over to Lucy, complaining, "I think my ass is broken." They hug, and it's a real hug, not a perfunctory pressing of shoulders, but the same hug they shared when Lucy dropped her at the airport two days ago. Almost an Astrid hug.

Lucy turns to greet Brian and suddenly Astrid is there. She looks a little pissed, and as she takes her turn squeezing the daylights out of Maxine she grumbles, "I hear from your sister you're on your way home? What the fuck is that?"

John is there, holding Star, as comfortably as if he's been doing it for years instead of days. They hug with the baby between them, and then he hands her to Maxine. Suddenly all is still as Maxine cradles Star and stares into her eyes. Maxine flashes to the photo of her holding Lucy, and she laughs as she holds out a finger and Star wraps her tiny fingers around it. Maxine is mesmerized.

"Hey you. Remember me?" she whispers.

They file into the bookstore and Maxine continues to stare at Star. "I missed you, little bug."

She feels a hand on her shoulder and a deep voice whispers in her own ear, "I missed you, too." Maxine turns to find Jay gazing down at her with an intensity that makes her knees go a little wobbly. Astrid scoops Star out of her arms and everyone seems to fade away as Maxine and Jay face each other.

Unsure what's appropriate here, they stare at each other like two high school freshman on a blind date. Maxine knows she's blushing. Jay grins and shoves his hand into his pockets, nodding in agreement to some unasked question.

"Hey," Maxine says.

"Hey," Jay replies.

Father Brian saves them. "Oh, for the love of God, does anyone here not know what these two are up to? Don't let us stop you from having a proper hello, please."

Jay folds Maxine in his arms, gently at first, then he tightens his hold and lifts her off her feet, turning to carry her away from the group, between the rows of books. When her feet touch the floor again, he kisses her, and she tastes him and smells him, and it's all exactly how she remembered it.

"I said a proper hello, not a total consummation,"

Brian calls out. "When you finish up, I need a ride home."

Maxine tears herself away from Jay and takes a minute to compose herself. Jay stays where he is as Maxine walks slowly back to Brian, trying to ignore the amusement of her friends. She puts a hand on each of Brian's shoulders and whispers into his ear, "Thank you. You're a good friend." Then she backs up and jokes, "I'm not sure I can spend five more minutes in the car with you."

Out of the corner of her eye, Maxine sees Astrid nudge John, who says, "Oh. Right. I'd be happy to drive you home."

Brian scowls at Maxine. "It was no picnic for me, either." Then he hugs her lightly and says quietly, "Be happy, Maxine."

When John returns from the short trip to Brian's parents' house, Lucy invites them upstairs to her apartment. Lucy has thrown together a welcome home happy hour, complete with trays of quesadillas, chicken satay, stuffed mushrooms, sweet potato fries and lots of beer and wine. Maxine doesn't know what to say when she walks into the dining room and sees the table laden with so much food. Lucy must have done it all at the last minute. She pours herself a glass of wine and corners Lucy in the kitchen while everyone else fills their plates.

"Lucy," she scolds, "you didn't have to do this."

"I did, actually. Astrid made me." Lucy smiles. "Don't worry, they helped. Besides, everyone wanted to see you." She frowns. "Mom doesn't know you're here yet, does she?"

"No, I couldn't quite handle that tonight. Why?"

"Because I didn't invite her. You're getting in tomorrow night, okay?"

Maxine nods. "Okay. Thanks, Lucy. Really."

"You're very welcome."

Maxine doubts these people have ever before been in one room together, but they fall into an easy banter. Maxine can't remember the last time she felt so relaxed. Looking around at Lucy, Astrid, John, Star and Jay, she realizes they are her new community. She has found her tribe, as surely as Star found hers during the baby's welcoming ceremony. She imagines her own tribe will grow over time, but for now it is just right, and she knows she is lucky to have finally landed where she belongs.

When Star begins to fuss and make hungry noises, Astrid nurses her and says they should probably get going once she's finished. Jay and John start making trips to unload Maxine's car, and Lucy and Maxine clear dishes and glasses and get started on loading the dishwasher and putting away leftover food. John grumbles about the countless book boxes and the freaking stairs, and both Lucy and Jay grin at Maxine.

When John announces, "That's the last of it, thank God," Maxine and Lucy join them in the extra bedroom, sparsely furnished with a futon, a dresser and a desk. Stacks of book boxes take up the better part of the wall with the dresser. Everything else is stacked in a corner.

"Thank you so much, guys. Luce, you sure you don't mind me taking over your office?" Maxine asks. "If you're having second thoughts, I'm sure they wouldn't mind taking it all back down."

John stalks out of the room without a word. Maxine walks over to her books, running her hands over the boxes, checking to make sure all are accounted for: A-D, E-G, and so on. When she turns, Lucy has left and she is alone with Jay. They smile at each other across the small room.

Astrid pokes her head in the door, Star snoozing in her sling. "Hey, John wants to go before you make him do any more physical stuff. Call me tomorrow."

Maxine crosses the room, hugs Astrid and kisses Star's nose. "Maybe I'll swing by?"

Astrid nods, grinning. "Welcome home, my friend." She waves at Jay, then leaves, closing the door softly behind her.

Maxine turns and walks slowly to Jay. He takes both of her hands in his and murmurs, "Hi there."

"Hi there." Maxine feels unsure of herself, no matter how enthusiastically he greeted her downstairs. This is the first time they've touched since then, as if neither was sure it was appropriate to behave as a couple in front of everyone. It was torture for Maxine, being so close. Now he tugs her gently to him until their bodies touch. She stares at his chest, close enough to smell him, then tilts her head back.

"I guess I should get going, too." He kisses her softly on the mouth and pulls away, letting go of her hands and wrapping his arms around her waist. She stands on her tiptoes to hug him and she thinks this is sweet, and smart, to not start anything right now. Then she turns her face to his and they kiss again, lightly at first. Before long

Soft Landing

Maxine runs her hands under his shirt to feel the skin of his back and chest and stomach, which she has been thinking about doing since she said good bye to him two days ago. He backs her against the wall and kisses her neck, cupping her breasts under her shirt. She can feel his hard-on against her hip, and she slips her hand into his jeans. He groans as she makes contact, but the next second he's not touching her anymore and he's pulling her hand away, pinning both hands against the wall behind her. They stare at each other, panting, and Maxine hopes he's trying to decide whether to screw her on the futon or the floor, or maybe up against the wall. But he shakes his head.

"Not like this. I want to wake up with you," he whispers into her ear.

This sends shivers down her entire body, but she says, "I can't. I want to stay with Lucy tonight." She's thought this through. In fact, during the drive, she bored Brian endlessly with her plan to make a fresh start, with her priorities in order. Yet now, with Jay pressed against her, she can't believe the words are actually coming out of her mouth.

"I know," Jay says, his lips on her forehead.

She thought she'd have to explain, but he just understands. This is why she loves him. He's a good man, who cares about the needs and feelings of others without having to be reminded. To Maxine, this is remarkable.

Jay backs away reluctantly, smiling down at her. "But you have to come over soon. Virginia is dying to meet you."

Maxine's mind suddenly tilts with uncertainty. Who the hell is Virginia? Are he and his ex-wife on such good terms that he wants her stamp of approval? Could Virginia be his daughter's name and he thinks it's time they meet? Could he already have another girlfriend and want to keep everything out in the open?

"I'm sorry, who's Virginia?" Maxine asks evenly.

"I got a dog. Well, she got me, really. She was on the front porch the day you left and wouldn't go away. I think she's still a puppy, maybe a little less than a year."

Maxine's world slowly rights itself, and she bursts out laughing. "What kind of name is Virginia for a dog?" She groans. "Please tell me she doesn't have a last name."

Jay grins wickedly and says, "Woof."

They kiss on the stairs outside the door. Maxine walks him to his car and they kiss some more. Eventually, they peel themselves apart, and Maxine watches him drive away until she can no longer see his taillights.

Once the house is in order, Maxine and Lucy contemplate one another from either end of the sofa.

"You could have gone with him," Lucy says.

"Maybe tomorrow. I'm exhausted." Maxine yawns.

Lucy smiles. "I guess so. That was a long trip, and with Brian, no less. What the hell did you two talk about for ten hours? Was it enough time to confess all your sins?"

Maxine laughs. She is tired, but a good tired. It's a wonderful feeling, this warm welcome. She never expected to end up back home after so many years, yet here she is. She knows her real journey began long before today, and the best part is that it's just beginning.

EPILOGUE

My dear Star,   *July 16, 2007*

Happy birthday, little bug! Your mother has been my best friend for as long as I can remember, and she has chosen me to be your "guidemother." It's a role I plan to take seriously. I'm a little late with this first letter, but I plan to write one every year on your birthday.

The first thing you should know is that you couldn't ask for better parents, and I promise I'm not just saying that because they're my friends. They are loving, funny, fun, cool people committed to making the world a better place. And they are completely, hopelessly in love with you! They will always do what's right for you, letting you be yourself while helping you grow into the best possible version of yourself.

In addition to your parents, you are surrounded by so many people who will love and nurture you. When you were brand new you had a "welcoming ceremony" that was one of the most beautiful things I have ever seen. So many people came to meet you and open their hearts to the newest little member of their community. Always know that you are part of a much larger family than your own, and we are here, looking out for you.

I'm so happy to be a part of your life. I'm eager to watch you grow and see who you will become. I will do anything I can to help you on that journey. When you need me, let me know and I will be there for you. Your arrival changed my life for the better, and I want my friendship to do the same for you.

So, my bright little Star, welcome to this wonderful world. We are going to have so much fun!

*All my love,
Maxine*